RABBIT IN THE MOON

RABBIT IN THE MOON

The Mexico Stories

KAREN BRENNAN

Schaffner Press

Library of Congress Control Number: 2023949878

ISBN: 978-1-639640-45-4 (Paperback)
ISBN: 978-1-639640-47-8 (PDF)
ISBN: 978-1-639640-46-1 (EPUB)

To Geoff, who loves these stories

and to Raquelita, who loves Mexico

The fable of the rabbit, which is on the moon, is this: It is said that the gods were mocking the moon, and slapped its face with a rabbit, and hence the rabbit remained marked on the face, darkening it, like a cardinal. Afterwards, the moon went out to light the world.

FROM *LA HISTORIA GENERAL DE LAS COSAS DE NUEVA ESPAÑA* (BERNARDINO DE SAHAGÚN, 1499-1590)

my friend the moon rises:
she is beautiful tonight, but when is she not beautiful?
LOUISE GLÜCK

CONTENTS

CITY: A PROLOGUE   1

BELLS   3

GABRIEL'S CHAIR   7

MISS AMERICAS   13

SACHA'S DOG   25

ECLIPSE   35

ZACK   45

TURISTA   63

RABBIT IN THE MOON   67

THE BEETLE AND THE NUN   75

AT THE FIGHTS   79

NUMBER FOUR   85

EVE'S HAIR, A CORRIDA   97

MAYA SUE   113

GHOSTS   119

THE RED ROOM   127

ART AND DEATH   133

JAKE'S WIFE   143

JULIAN'S BIRDS   153

THE SWAYING SHADOW   177

RABBIT IN THE MOON

CITY: *A PROLOGUE*

I USED TO DREAM of a city. The avenues curved and slanted upwards around buildings which were blurred but spired. When it rained, I could see visions gathered in the shallow bowls between stones. My face transformed into an animal, a tree, a cloud.

I knew every inch of this city and dreamt of it for weeks at a time. In the dream I'd simply be walking around. I'd be witness to the fact of the city rising on either side of me, and in front, upon the dark horizon. The cobbled streets; the pink walls that turned orange in the rain; the light which in moonlight or during the day was always the same—gray and gold, a calmer version from my childhood.

I'd be walking down familiar streets, following a familiar route, but I had no destination. At times they'd light the lamps but this warm artificial light would not affect the predominant light which was the same gray-gold. Once I saw a bird fall through the sky in spasms. Another time I wandered up the staircase of a municipal building.

After my face becomes a cloud it drifts into an animal again. My heart may have been broken in this city. I have no way of knowing since I encounter no one familiar. There are times when I feel I am about to recognize someone and so I walk with a certain deliberation and try to stay alert. For example, I am walking down the highway which runs parallel to the railroad track and I have the sense that someone I know intimately is trying to overtake me. But when I turn around the street is empty, and a light is breaking through the sky in the shape of the sea.

Incessantly, everywhere, are cathedral bells chiming but the spires are blurred. This is because I look up only occasionally and so it must be that my eyes are not used to such heights. Once, looking, I saw a clock, and this frightened me. Otherwise I am glad to be here. When, as has happened for long periods, I am away from the city, I do not miss it. But when I close my eyes and there it is pushing into the life of my dream, I feel the full weight of my yearning for it, as if I had not known what I wanted until the moment of returning.

Therefore, this city is connected to my inmost desires. Like the spires they are not clear to me, even as they are passed in these streets and viewed from below in their gray golden haze.

Nothing will ever happen here. It is as though the history of the city is complete without my participation. In this sense, the city is a book whose pages have been written and I am the reader who wanders through its stories.

BELLS

AT IRREGULAR INTERVALS THE bell tolls. It tolls eight times and then it may toll seventeen times a while later, at no particular hour. Occasionally it tolls twenty-one times, waits a beat or two, and just when you feel you are drifting off to sleep, it tolls once more, a single hard resonance of iron on iron clanging into the dead of night, into the motionless air and the stultifying heat and the whine of mosquitos.

There may be a man ringing the bell, we imagine, standing in the belfry at all hours, night and day, his life devoted to ringing the bells of the cathedral as some are devoted to shopping or travel. I ring the bell when I want to, he tells his wife who brings him his meals in a brown sack. Lately, she has been conveying the complaints of the tourists as well, who are irritated by the irregularity imposed upon their lives by the caprice of the bellringer. *What's with the bell? There seems to be no purpose except to annoy us.*

The man, Jose, looks thoughtful. He talks to his wife with his mouth full of bread. The bell has no purpose, eh? he says to his wife, call her Renaldia. He is wearing Levi's and a vintage Beatles tee shirt with missing sleeves. His biceps and pectorals are overly developed in proportion to the rest of his body since it takes tremendous strength to ring the bells. First, he must swing his body over a parapet; then holding the long rope to which the heaviest bell is attached (400 pounds), he positions himself on the stone ledge overlooking the city. Generally he pulls four ropes at once, each attached to bells of differing weights, and what this produces is not, as one would expect, the sound of multiple bells ringing, but an impression of unadulterated clarity on the listener, a brief conviction that time indeed will not pass but is doomed to the moment and its endless reiteration of itself.

At first, as a teenager, Jose had neither the strength nor the will to ring the four bells at once. In those days, he was happy to be punctual, to mark the Angeles, Matins, Compline, and so forth. But something happened to him to make him have contempt for punctuality; it was as if the bells themselves had overtaken him, as if their rhythms were purer and more accurate than time itself—because, he reasons, if time is ignored perhaps it follows logically that we will live forever. But he keeps his idea to himself and does not share it even with Renaldia, who would not understand.

Lately she has been growing a little moustache and its appearance, like two faint smudges of ash above her lip, fills her with foreboding. She worries that she is changing into another person, that bad fortune has suddenly flapped in her direction, wafting away the old Renaldia and dragging forth this new one with a moustache.

There had been a time, actually, when she had been more patient with Jose who was, everyone knew, impractical and anti-social, who preferred his hours spent in the belfry, surrounded by stone and echoes and staggering perspectives, to an evening in his casita with Renaldia and her mother and their three or four children—he couldn't keep track—milling around his knees. He prefers loneliness to society, a long view to a myopic one, and the ringing of bells which seem to him to mark, instead of time, that which is more unsettled—a cloud's passing, for example, or the death of a dog or a boy's sneeze. And Renaldia had understood this as a wife will always understand the quirks and shortcomings of her dear husband compared to, say, Martin Gonzalez, who plays baseball with his kids on weekends and cooks enchilada sauce from scratch.

But these days Renaldia's understanding is wearing thin. There is the fact of the moustache, for one thing, which seems to announce a change in her relationship with Jose, indeed a change in life itself, because what is an omen if not profound, its power extending beyond itself? So Renaldia, instead of proffering silently and without judgment the lunches and dinners that Jose requires, instead of mounting peacefully the 223 steps that lead to the little room where more often than not Jose can be seen squatting and peering at slivers of the city between the chinks of stone, this Renaldia is liable to stomp gracelessly up the long flight of stairs with fury in her heart. Then she sets the meal in front of Jose with a noisy clatter and proceeds to contribute to the disturbance herself, complaining to Jose about his absence, the lack of money for children's clothes, her mother's annoying habits, the filthy air, how the TV has terrible static, et cetera. When she exhausts these personal topics, she moves to a litany of the complaints of others—the maestro at the children's school who needs a new truck, his Uncle Tonio whose filling fell out of his tooth, and winding up with our complaints, the complaints of the tourists to whom time is nothing if not everything and so are particularly vulnerable to any fluctuation of the day's activities.

Lastly, when Jose's impassive face has darkened and his eyes have drifted away, because for only so long is he able to listen before his own thoughts, so familiar and comforting, in their large vague shapes, intervene, at this point Renaldia points to her moustache which, she claims, has been sent to punish her for losing control of her husband. Clearly, I am turning into the man of the family because the man of the family has flown the coop! And what if it grows darker and bushy, then what? What will your brother, Mr. Macho, say? And how about my mother, do you ever in your selfish life think of her, Jose, her own daughter with a moustache curling up at the ends and who knows maybe a beard next?

Understand, it's not that Jose isn't moved by the appeals of Renaldia or even that he isn't compassionate about the moustache which, he would have to agree, is a bit off-putting. Rather, it is that, like a priest or an artist, like anyone with a vocation, Jose cannot stop doing what he has been doing. No more than he can stop the ideas about time and eternity from rolling into his mind like a lustrous fog. We imagine him thinking: *At this minute in this city everything may have changed and the day that was yesterday might be today and who knows where today is.* And this is how it goes night after night, through the sticky heat of May and the torrential downpours of June where the rainfall sounds more like bodies and furniture plummeting to earth and where the bells peal intermittently, invading our dreams like life.

GABRIEL'S CHAIR

L ET'S SAY YOU ARE going to visit Gabriel. You may want
to talk to him, or just hang out, look at his paintings and drink
beer. There in his kitchen are two chairs. Both are wicker with painted
wooden frames. The only difference between them is that one of them
is broken. The broken one is not broken in such a way that it is lopsided
on the floor and needs a matchbook to set it straight. In fact, if you look
at its placement on the floor on the other side of a low table with a little
embroidered cloth and a few ashtrays and places for glasses of beer, you
would almost be fooled into believing the chair is not broken. But actually
the wicker on the chair has quite obviously shredded and so if you sit on
it, which you must, inevitably, because this is the chair you are offered, one
half of your ass will fall through almost to the floor and the other half will
rest upon what is left of the wicker and the frame itself, so that you can
actually sit on this chair for a short while, but you will not be comfortable.
Thus, I am calling this story "Gabriel's Chair."

Perhaps this story has also to do with a deeper level of discomfort in Gabriel's presence.

So there you are sitting on Gabriel's chair. Gabriel is sitting across from you in the good chair, and he is laughing. Whether he is laughing because he can see the half of your ass falling through the chair or because he can see you struggling to maintain a look of comfort and ease despite your half an ass falling through to the floor or whether he is laughing because he is on the good chair and you're not is not clear to you.

When Gabriel laughs he shows his teeth and he crinkles his eyes. But Gabriel's laugh is not a full laugh. It is not the laugh of one who is accustomed to laughing a lot and heartily. There is a little strain to it, as if the laugh had to struggle against a contradictory impulse—perhaps a more instinctive urge to shout angrily.

You are conversing about poetry. Poetry, says Gabriel, is not the universal language. Painting is.

You disagree. There is no universal language, you say. Poetry and painting each have their own sets of problems.

Do you want some more beer? asks Gabriel. He pours from the quart bottle of Corona and what you get is mostly foam. It's ok, you say, because you weren't planning on drinking much with Gabriel this afternoon. For one thing, it's hot today and in his little room it's even hotter than outside because Gabriel has closed the curtains so the light won't hit his eyes.

The foam is fine, you say.

That's not a real beer, says Gabriel with a touch of scorn.

In a way, you've come to admire Gabriel's scorn. It hits you flat in the stomach every time, bullseye. It is, therefore, an exemplary scorn, perfectly conceived and perfectly aimed.

Meanwhile your ass is beginning to feel more or less captured in the frame of the wicker chair. You have the urge to get up and go outside. You want to wander around, you tell Gabriel. I get my best ideas wandering, you say. You are wander woman, he says and then he laughs at his joke.

Have you ever noticed you are the one who laughs the hardest at your jokes? you ask Gabriel. He laughs with his mouth wide open so that he actually makes a sound like ha ha ha.

Drink some rum with me, he says.

But you need to paint, you say.

Don't tell me what I need to do, he says.

Your conversations with Gabriel often take this odd turn. Whether you stay or go you are entangled in complications. Be careful of your language, he says.

Then it occurs to you that Gabriel has this chair for just this purpose, to encourage people to cut their visits short. Even though it is pulled so cozily up to the little table and seems, except for the damaged seat, to be so appealing, facing the other chair in an inviting way and within easy reach of the table with its embroidered cloth and the glasses of beer and the seashell ashtray.

I must fix that chair someday, says Gabriel, absently, when you stand up.

Here is the point I was trying to make, says Gabriel. The people in Chiapas all have eyes, but not all of them can read.

True, you say. But do they have eyes for Jackson Pollack? Do they have eyes for Mark Rothko?

All art exists in an historical context, you say. You feel you are right and your righteousness gives your voice a certain inflection that you find distressing. You've heard it before in the voices of others and here it is in your voice. I'm not saying you don't have a point, you say.

I'm a little hungry, you say. Do you happen to have any crackers or bread? Nada, says Gabriel. But I have rum. Rum isn't what I'm thinking about right now, you say. Why not? says Gabriel.

Gabriel has two chairs, one broken, one small table, one square embroidered cloth, a stove, no fridge, a mattress with a gray blanket, a TV, several easels, many paintings and paint cans and brushes and tubes of paint. He has a quart of Corona. He has two glasses, a shell for an ashtray, a painted stone on his wall, a photo of his mother, a terrace covered with plants, geraniums, peppers and beans, a rooftop over the terrace that you climb to on a little ladder. He has a quart of rum, but no Coke.

No cigarettes, no TV, no washing machine and dryer, no fridge, no stereo. No closets, no bathtub, no crackers, no bread.

It's impossible to translate a poem, he announces. Prose is different, he says. You can get to the meaning in prose.

How so? you say. The Corona, as warm as it is, is strangely refreshing and you've begun to feel relaxed and convivial. You don't want to argue this question of language with Gabriel, but it seems unavoidable.

There is a bird shrieking at the window and around your head a mean looking wasp has begun to circle. I'm allergic to those things, you say, referring to the wasp. Gabriel says: There is no way to get close to the meaning of a poem in another language. It has to be a different poem, and so the original is lost.

In some sense, you agree, the original is lost. But if it's a good translation the spirit, the heart of the poem, is conveyed. I like that new painting, by the way, you add, because while you've been talking to Gabriel you've been looking over his head at his latest painting of a naked woman seated on a very comfortable looking gold bean bag chair with her legs open, proudly displaying her crotch. What you like most about this painting is the checkered floor background which has little pieces of the sky in each square. You also admire the way he's drawn in the woman's genitalia, with great care and delicacy. You tell him this.

Genitalia? he says, laughing very hard. Well? you say. What should I say? It's so scientific, he says. Why don't you just say *pussy*? Whatever, you say. Now you have made me lose the very important point I was making, he says. You have distracted me. I thought I was the one making the very important point, you say. No, he says, I was about to say something very, very important and now I've lost my train of thought.

Well, you say, I should be going. Because now that you've sat down on the chair again your ass is squeezing out of the bottom in what you are sure must be a very obscene manner and you think it's time for your wandering around and thinking. Also, you have a long walk home, up an irregular stone staircase that has one hundred stairs, next to the oldest iglesia in the city where the bells sound like pots and pans instead of bells.

You don't have to go, he says. We could drink rum. We could drink rum, you agree, but we have no Coke.

Gabriel has no Coke and no condoms. You know this from experience. He thinks you should bring the condoms, but you have no condoms either. You have no idea where to buy condoms in this city or how to say condoms in his language. There are times when you fool yourself into thinking you know how to speak his language and at those times you string all the words you know together and try to force your meaning into them. But Gabriel interrupts. Stop. I don't understand one word you are saying. Speak in English, please, and speak clearly and precisely because remember English is not my first language. Gabriel derives a certain pleasure in these admonitions, but he has a point nonetheless, you feel. Your Spanish is lousy and the idea of buying condoms should probably be abandoned. Anyway, you are not planning to have sex with Gabriel anymore. His passionate face, his eyes that crinkle at the sides, his soft hands with their skin like silk, his beautiful brown body and its shadows and arches and planes and treacheries are no longer of interest. You would rather sit on his broken chair and watch him laugh at you: ha ha ha.

Maybe you will use his laughter in this story and you will have the last laugh. Therefore, "Gabriel's Chair" will be symbolic of his lack of hospitality, his enjoyment of your discomfort, his need to put you off balance so that he can experience a small measure of superiority at your expense.

Communication is always hard, you say, in any language, painting or poetry or English or Spanish. Yes, he says, I agree with you. Finally I agree with you. Then he leans back in his chair and together you watch the sunlight fill the curtains and slide over the geranium leaves on the window sill. There are no blooms.

They have lost their hearts, says Gabriel, referring to the geraniums.

At this point in time, you tell Gabriel, I myself have a cold heart. This is a lie, but you feel you need protection from Gabriel. You feel if you say the words, they will come true.

Gabriel takes a long swallow of beer. He sets his glass on the table and wipes his mouth with the back of his hand. Then he looks you straight in the eye: How does it feel to have a cold heart? he asks. Amazing, you say. As usual, you put too much faith in language.

MISS AMERICAS

A T TEN A.M. MARIANNE ascends from her well-appointed Hotel Casa Mantilla Negra bed and makes her unsteady way to the window because there is a tremendous amount of noise, clanging of garbage trucks and taxis and people actually screeching and birds cawing and cathedral bells all out of tune. She is pissed. Her husband, a tire magnate, sleeps soundly in his own bed, fully dressed in a golf shirt and orange slacks and blue and white argyle socks and brown shoes, and his snores contribute to the rest of the racket which has disturbed Marianne in the dream wherein her brother offers her a very distinctive silk scarf and asks for a small sum of money in exchange. But she feels his price is fishy, she feels uneasy about handing over to him the 25 pesos. She feels that in doing so she will actually lose more than she gains, which in reality doesn't make much sense. Also, she hasn't seen or even communicated with her brother in years.

Now she is at the elegantly arched window of the exclusive Casa Mantilla Negra and she is looking at the street expecting to see the source of all this racket in a whirling colorful scene. But, as if someone had pressed the pause button, all she sees are two burros with flour sacks strapped to their haunches and their owners, skinny men with moustaches, talking and spitting intermittently. And the bells are ringing, of course. The interminable bells.

With a flourish Marianne closes the drapes—these are the long silk-lined damask drapes of the upscale Hotel Casa Mantilla Negra—and she wanders to the gilded full-length mirror where she surveys herself with a bit of admiration and an equal bit of regret. In her long white nightdress bordered with white embroidered fleur de lis and little edges of lace at the cuffs and hem, Marianne is still gorgeous at 50. Her cheekbones are high and sharp as daggers, her neck slopes gracefully, her black, lustrous hair pours to her shoulders, with a stunning silver strand running through it now and then. She has managed, with the aid of stringent diets and workouts, to keep the same figure that dazzled the judges in the 60s—the long legs, the high perfect breasts, the erect and dignified posture. Her nose has not begun to grow. She has laugh lines, true, but none of those deep folds on either side of the mouth and nose and none of those tragic vertical lip lines caused by smoking or talking too much. Marianne limits herself to necessary words—pass the salt, how much?, I have a headache—and does not engage in idle chatter of any kind. Once she was Miss Americas.

Still, at the same time and regretfully, Marianne cannot get away from the fact of her age. She sees its subtle signs meandering across her body even as the world sees an extraordinarily attractive woman in, perhaps, her early 40s. It is her misfortune to notice, for example, a small discoloration on her cheek, and that one nipple is now noticeably larger than the other. She tries to repress knowledge of these things, but it's difficult in this day and age with Nieman Marcus models wandering around the exclusive Casa Mantilla Negra, arranging themselves on the old stone walls or near the tiled pool in their chic combat boots and skinny tights and chiffon blouses.

The tire magnate, whose name is George, sleeps soundly, his snore scurrying into the room like a hungry rat and then scurrying out again. Marianne herself is starved. Lately, this has been happening to her: terrible uncontrollable hunger. Where she used to fantasize about being caressed and even screwed by Robert Redford, she now fantasizes about food, vast amounts of food. She sits on her bed and surveys George whose earlobes are sprouting little hairs and whose mouth is partially opened like the mouth of an idiot, emitting now and then a thin line of drool, and she imagines eating her way through a chocolate cake without utensils, shoving it in her mouth with both hands, licking the icing from the platter.

She wishes she could sleep. That she could return to the dream of her brother and the silk scarf, if only to puzzle out that negotiation, but George's snoring has now gone into another register. It is louder, the snorting that accompanies each inhale, a series of glottal, mechanical clicks and the exhales puffy and strained sounding, like farts. Suddenly, once again, the street is full of people, someone is playing a trumpet which clashes with the bells and a group of tourists are arguing stridently in English. This is too much for one person to bear, says Marianne aloud, and she sheds her nightgown and pulls on a pair of stone-washed jeans and a black blouse. I am only going out, she says loudly to George, but the tire magnate twitches a shoulder in response to this announcement.

———

Last night they'd been out drinking. First one bar, then another bar, etc., etc., etc. They all looked vaguely the same. One bar had a band, the other had a guitarist, the third had a guitarist and a violinist, the fourth had a jazz combo with a saxophonist and a woman singer. At each place they drank shots of expensive tequila, salting slivers of lime and sucking them and then downing the tequila. They became very drunk and then they had an argument in the street. Why are you always insisting on getting drunk every time we go away? Marianne asked the tire magnate her husband. Me? he said. I'm not the one. It's you who always suggests we go out and do something, go out and meet people, whereas I would be just as happy— here he stopped mid-sentence and looked up at the moon which was full and very bright, and he looked up at it as if a miracle—a UFO or flying saucer—had occurred in the sky, and he drew in his breath.

Now what? said Marianne, now you can't even finish your own sentences? But George could not tear his eyes from the moon which he looked at as if for the first time. He noticed craters—he'd always heard of craters—which must be the blue ragged circles around the grayish holes; and he noticed the way the light seeped from the moon and spread into the sky in dense, milky spools; and he noticed the shape of the moon which seemed to him to be the prototype for the shapes he loved the most—tires and breasts.

What do I have to do to get your attention George? Marianne was saying and she was a little upset because it appeared to her that something was wrong with George. She thought he might be having a mental or physical collapse of some kind, because truthfully he was not getting any younger and this was about the time of life that one could expect such things. When she punched him on the arm and said George he turned to her with a puzzled look on his face, as if he were not quite sure who she was. It's so beautiful, he said. How much do you think they would take for it?

Idioto, George, it's the moon for Christ's sake. It's not for sale.

Then, on the way home, the taxi broke down. The driver, who was wearing a yellow baseball cap and wooden beads around his neck, crouched under the opened hood, his baseball cap perched at the edge of his head, intently studying the innards of the car in a way that did not make Marianne hopeful. All this time, George was looking out of the window with a dazed expression on his face and every once in a while Marianne had to punch him on the arm and say George, snap out of it. Then he'd say,

Do you think a million would do it? It's not a great location, you know. George, said Marianne, don't talk to me, you've lost your mind, and she stared out the opposite window and tried to ignore the fact of her husband who was obviously deteriorating before her eyes.

Then there was a storm, and thunder roared and lightning cracked and Marianne could tell from the timing between the thunder and the lightning that the lightning was very close. And here was the taxi driver still hovering over the car's engine while water poured into it. Finally he returned to the cab where Marianne was seething both at her husband who continued to gaze dreamily out of the window, even though there was nothing to see on account of the streams of rain falling from the sky, and at the taxi driver who was obviously very stupid to stand out there in a rain storm and allow his engine to fill with water. It won't work, the cab driver informed Marianne sadly, as he returned to the driver's seat and lit a cigarette. I wish you wouldn't smoke, said Marianne. It's bad enough I have to get stuck in this cab with you until god knows when.

Agreeably, the taxi driver stubbed the cigarette in the ashtray and turned up the radio. And I wish you'd turn down that radio, said Marianne. Sssh, said the taxi driver. This is very important, it's politics. Because on the radio a newscaster was discussing the upcoming elections with a guest:

Newscaster: And so you're telling me you think the process will be so closely monitored that there's no way in the world to fix the election.

Guest: That's what I believe. I have made a careful study and in my opinion, which you can take or leave, but which I give you with the assurance of my honor and my life, in the name of Cuauhtemoc, that the process will be fair. (Here the guest raises his voice in an impassioned manner.) I say you have my word for it!

Newscaster: Yes, well, we know how much that's worth, don't we, Senator _____.

I hate this, said Marianne, and I insist that you turn it off or down. I have no interest whatsoever in politics, which are boring. At this George dropped his head on her shoulder and began to snore loudly. I'll bet, said the taxi driver. You and your kind are bored by the oppression of the masses, I suppose. Me and my kind? said Marianne. The oppression of the masses? You honestly believe that the masses are oppressed in this day and age? Give me a break.

At which the taxi driver turned the radio even louder and made an impatient movement with his hand for her to leave the cab and walk home in the rain. The masses should get off their butts! she screamed, nevertheless. The masses should stop whining! And the newscaster was saying, Do you honestly expect me to believe that you, Senator _____, are a disinterested party in this affair? And the guest was saying, I have no control of course, señor, over your system of beliefs, but I am telling you with my life and heart, that I want only to see justice tempered with mercy prevail in our country, and to that end I have pledged myself.

Here George jolted awake on her shoulder wearing an exceedingly silly smile. Marianne, he said, gliding his hand over her breast and giving it a squeeze. I have been dreaming that we moved to a far-off place. Very far away. His eyes were dreamy as he slid his hand beneath her blouse and tried unsuccessfully to fondle her inside the padded bra. This is the last straw, said Marianne, wrenching herself away. You are all making me crazy. At this the taxi driver broke into loud laughter and George, looking only a little baffled, joined in. Then, amazingly, the cab started up.

———

Twenty-five years ago, when Marianne won the Miss Americas competition, her life changed. Before that she'd been a country girl with a good figure who, like the other girls in the village, spent most of her time having a crush on this or that boy and looking in the mirror. Then there was a local beauty contest, then a state, then a national and at each level she held her head with more dignity and she began actually to feel that she deserved to be worshipped and honored, so that even before the decision of the final judges was reached, Marianne had developed the imperious, slightly aggrieved air which has held her in good stead all her life. Now when she walks down the streets of this small, charming city, she is a queen. Her breasts are commanding under the black blouse and her stone-washed, artfully torn jeans cling charmingly to her long legs. She is aware of the effect she creates as she walks past which is to cause people to stop whatever they are doing and follow her respectfully with their eyes until she disappears from view. There was a time when this annoyed her, at the height of her career as international beauty queen, but now as she ages she is, she has to admit, addicted to the scrutiny of others, which is to say she is addicted to herself as a fantasy and has acquired the long habit of seeing herself through the appreciative eyes of others.

But she is hungry and isn't it ironic that this very hunger is what threatens to speed up the demise of Marianne's beauty because sadly she is developing a little belly which nothing, not even special Spanx, will completely diminish. And still—this is what amazes her—even walking down the street and thinking of this unattractive jiggle of flesh clamped beneath her jeans, and seeing in her mind's eye the first signs of under-arm flab and a noticeable thickening of the waistline, even through all of this, her appetite will not abate. Contrario, it seems this hunger grows fiercer the more she thinks about the tragedy of her own body; even as she conjures up double chins and small piggy eyes lost in the flesh of a face, even then, she is with the other parts of her mind thinking about the cheese omelette and frijoles she would love to devour at the Buen Café. But then the cheerless vision of the Nieman Marcus models posed against the old stone walls of the exclusive Casa Mantilla Negra glides into her mind to counteract her hunger and right then she plans to ask George to take her picture in the same spot. She will wear her short white shorts and her polka dot halter top which is more appealing than combat boots and baggy shirts, let's face it. And she will now buy a special lens for the expensive, professional camera, her birthday present to George.

———

The camera store is small and dark and a tall rack crammed with exorbitantly priced postcards stands awkwardly in front of the counter. Marianne has gone through this postcard selection before, most of them mounted photographs of cathedrals and old doors shot in a dreary light. Camera slung over her shoulder in its leather case, she edges herself between the rack and the counter and requests the lens she needs from the blind proprietor whose face never ceases to give her a chill, the eyes squeezed way back in the sockets so that only a slice of pale gray light shows through. They remind her of a certain kind of narrow and inedible fish from her childhood. Nevertheless, he is very adroit at choosing the correct lens from a big shelf filled with specialty lenses, removing her camera from its case and demonstrating how to adjust the lens and attach it to her camera. Then she turns around, a half turn really, and she hears the postcard rack clatter to the floor sending postcards everywhere, hundreds of them, all the cathedrals and doors. What is it? says the blind proprietor. Who is there? He gropes nervously in the air in front of him. Is it the postcards? I'm very sorry, she tells him, but this was not my fault. Your rack is off balance, she says, and as she says this she has the misfortune to have her sunglasses slide from the top of her head and fall to the floor next to the postcards. What have you done now? asks the proprietor irritably. What else has gone off balance for you?

For the next half hour she is sorting postcards while the proprietor stands by with his arms folded, a disapproving frown on his large, blind face. I said I was sorry, she says, arranging the postcards in stacks, cathedrals and doors, cathedrals and doors, and sounding to her own ears like a petulant child and not at all like the regal ex-beauty queen that she is in reality.

What you bend you must buy, he says, uncannily lifting a cathedral with a tiny dent in the corner. Ok, ok, how much? she says because by now all she wants to do is leave and forget this situation with the blind proprietor and postcards. She is disturbed in a way which is not even remotely familiar because since she left her small town all those many years ago no one has had the nerve to speak to her in the manner of this blind proprietor. At that moment, he reminds her of her father who also never noticed her great beauty but seemed to look right through her to some secret ugliness at the root of her being.

Three hundred, he says, holding out his palm, and she crumples up the note and thrusts it at him and leaves with fifteen dented postcards, all of the same cathedral with a black background.

Outside, tears spring to her eyes and she reaches under her sunglasses to dab them. Never has she been spoken to in such a manner; why did she put up with it? She has the urge to return to the shop without announcing herself and knock down his rack again. Or maybe she should make George speak to this man in a rough way and threaten to close his business. The whole time these vengeful thoughts are creeping into her mind, she is weeping and finally her shoulders are shaking with her gulps and sniffles and she takes refuge under a doorway where she hopes she won't be noticed.

———

But, of course, she is noticed because how could you not notice a beautiful woman sitting in a doorway weeping, clutching a camera in its leather case and an envelope of dented cathedrals? Who notices her is a dirty child in a dirty dress the color of iron filings who with her dirty hand outthrust begs for a peso. No, says Marianne, Vete, get out, she says. But

the child whose face wears the practiced abjection of her class and occu-
pation is persistent. Una peso, señora, she says, drawing out the syllables,
inflecting them in such a way that each seems dipped in oil and fake
misery, a misery which seems to mock the true misery of Marianne who
finally out of exhaustion fumbles in her bag for a peso, anything, to get
rid of this child with her mournful eyes and her dress which is ripped at
the hem and several sizes too small. She pulls out her compact and her
lip liner and several credit card receipts and the plastic tube where the
film has been, but there is no change at all at the bottom of her bag, only
shreds of an old Kleenex and a bobby pin.

No, she says, and she motions for the child to be on her way. No hay.

Then it seems to her the child's eyes lose their expression and become
inscrutable, gazing past her into the distance of the street where a white
dog with a spiral tail crosses and a tourist with a guitar makes his way
slowly up the hill. With an air of resignation, she sits on the stoop beside
the beauty queen whose tears have so recently been shed and draws her
bony knees to her chest and rests her chin on her palms. The cathedral bells
chime and a taxi rumbles by and a bird flies to the corner of a building
and flicks its feathers and the tourist with the large stomach reaches the
crest of the hill, within inches of the faces of the girl and the woman, both
wearing the same expression of weariness as if life has no more surprises
but bad ones.

What do you want? asks Marianne finally. Que Quieres? She opens
her purse and again removes one by one and with a great furious show
the lipstick, compact, credit card receipts, shred of Kleenex, and bobby
pin to demonstrate to the child once and for all that what she wants is an
impossibility. But amazingly the child smiles and points to the lipstick.
Quiero, she says. I want that.

———

And what could I do but give it to her? she tells George over lunch. Pearl Adder. You can only get it in the States at the Lancôme counter in Bloomingdale's. Frankly George, this vacation has been a bust. She is eating a large plate of nouvelle enchiladas prepared especially by the upscale staff at the Casa Mantilla Negra and for dessert she will have the profiteroles and champagne.

George, nursing a hangover, is eating scrambled eggs and watching a Nieman Marcus model in a tan trench coat and an orange silk scarf with very long legs.

George, your mind is a million miles away, she says. Pay attention, I want you to speak to that blind idiot in the camera store.

Yes dear, says George, patting her hand.

And take your eyes off that slut, she says, but just as she says it she notices something that shocks her. Look George, that scarf! She points to the model.

That is the very scarf my brother tried to sell me in last night's dream!

Shall I buy it for you? asks George.

That isn't the point, she says, and she struggles to remember the other details of the dream.

The model floats by, like a cloud, a swan. Young, beautiful (she is a honey blond with brown eyes), the drift of her hair against her cheek, the way she pivots on the point of her black shoe, all are signs that point to somewhere—but where?

Is this life a dream? she asks George.

I agree with you absolutely, my love, says George. He belches softly into the exclusive Casa Mantilla Negra gold-threaded napkin.

His wife, the former Miss Americas, is scooping profiterole between her immaculate teeth, but her eyes are fixed on the model, the scarf fluttering with indifference at her neck, as if it had no awareness of being transported from the dream world to this one.

SACHA'S DOG

THERE IS A LITTLE dog that belongs to Sacha and we see it here and there walking the streets like a human being with a destination. More often than not it is in search of Sacha who is getting drunk and then falling asleep some place. Sacha's dog, who is golden haired and as small as a cat, with a pointed face and ears like mittens, is no familiar breed, even as a mutt it is not familiar.

The dogs here are different from the dogs in other places mainly because they have been allowed to roam the urban streets for centuries and one senses they have evolved in ways that please them as opposed to ways which please the human population. They strike us as a bit uncanny, these dogs, as if they were scaling the edges of their species, about to transform themselves into some other creature.

This dog, the dog of Sacha, does not strictly speaking belong to Sacha; that is to say, Sacha didn't purchase this dog or find this dog and then decide to feed it. This dog, like most of the dogs in the city, is entirely self-reliant in the matter of food and entertainment. It loves Sacha, this is clear, and when Sacha is off on a long drunk the dog is disconsolate for a while, wandering anxiously trying to ascertain Sacha's whereabouts.

Tonight Sacha is at the cantina dancing with a woman with long hair. He does not know her name and thinks he will probably not ask because she is obviously a gringa and communication becomes so frustrating. Also, he is very drunk. He has been drinking margaritas and beer for three days and also smoking a little pot, and he is happy to dance to the salsa band and shut his eyes and groove with the music. The dog, who is nameless to humans at least, has no idea where Sacha is, but at this moment decides to try the cantina where the doorman, recognizing the dog, steps politely aside to allow it entrance. When it spots Sacha on the dance floor with the long-haired woman it gives a sharp yelp which Sacha recognizes as the signal for him to call it a day.

On the way home, Sacha is so drunk he stops every once in a while to get his bearings by holding onto a wall or the side of some building. Also, he takes a piss on the street. The dog is very long suffering during all of this and only nudges Sacha once when it appears he might fall asleep in a doorway against a green door. At his own door, which is black, he fumbles with his key and with the lock. Then he drops his keys and they fall into a grating. With his bad eyes at night, he has to pull up the grating and rummage in a pile of leaves. This is when the dog proves invaluable, ferreting out the keys in the pile of leaves and holding them out to Sacha with its teeth. Soon they are inside, the dog curled in a corner of the room on the cool tiles and Sacha lying horizontally across the bed with his clothes on.

Why does the dog love Sacha? Does Sacha play catch with the dog? Does he enter the dog in beauty contests? Does he send the dog to school or buy the dog doggie treats or make sure the dog has a nice flea collar? None of the above. Nor is he especially affectionate with the dog in other simpler ways; he hardly ever scratches the dog on the neck nor does he feed the dog scraps. But the dog loves Sacha in the neurotic, overbearing way that most people love their pets. It worries about Sacha, worries that he might get into a bar fight and lose all his teeth like Gabriel and worries that he will forget to feed himself. Many of his companions—and other perros in the city—tolerate this rather unconventional attitude in their friend, but to them it is strange to want to mingle so intimately with another species unless there is a payoff of some kind. But Sacha's dog is an altruist and expects no recompense for its trouble. The reward is in the deed itself, the feeling of peace it gives.

I am a satisfied dog, that's all I can say about it, he tells his friend, the white dog with the spiraled tail. I do what I can for Sacha and I think without me he'd actually be pretty lost. I'm grateful to have this chance. Here he pauses with a degree of smugness unbecoming in a dog. And so the white dog merely nods and smiles a little insincerely, because none of this makes sense to him and he secretly thinks this dog, his old friend, is possibly unbalanced.

Now Sacha is lying on the bed horizontally, with his clothes on. The dog would prefer Sacha to be under the covers with his shoes lined up neatly against the wall, but what can it do? It only has so much influence, especially when Sacha is drunk. It is content to have gotten this far with Sacha after his three-day binge. When there's a knock at the door and some shouting at the stoop, the dog doesn't think twice about it, he feels sure that Sacha is unconscious enough that he will not be disturbed. The knocking continues, louder, as if somebody began by pounding the door with their fists and wound up by pounding it with a hatchet. The dog gives a long sigh and goes to nudge Sacha awake. But Sacha is presently having a dream about the woman with the long hair who is riding a horse in the mist and he is the cowboy with the lasso on a sand dune and then he is at his mother's house and she is feeding him ice cream, and then he is at the beach with his childhood friend, Jose the bell ringer, and they are throwing stones into the sea. Sacha has never actually seen the sea, but in his dream it is green with little specks of orange shot through it and covered with rolling waves that look like the white scalloped hems of his sisters' communion dresses. He is experiencing great happiness being at the sea with Jose and suddenly in the moment of throwing a flat purple stone, he realizes he is dreaming and turns to Jose so they can laugh together about this miracle of meeting in a dream, at which point Jose throws a stone at Sacha's head and he wakes up with the dog thumping its tail in his eye and to the sounds of people hammering at his door and shouting his name and other profanities.

The people who are visiting Sacha are his friend Tonio and some others who happened to be passing by at this hour. Don't you have any beer Sacha you son of a bitch, what's wrong with you? There are two men counting Tonio and one woman and the woman, Rosa, is wearing cutoff blue jeans and a Guatemalan vest with nothing underneath. Sacha can see her small breasts, the nipples dark brown and protruding at the tips. It excites Sacha to glimpse them through the gaps under her arms and he gives Tonio a knowing look when the woman's back is turned.

The friend winks and says loudly, Rosa, Sacha thinks you're hot stuff. I didn't say that, says Sacha, but he is laughing, embarrassed, and he opens his refrigerator and says again, I don't have any beer, maybe some rum. Rum is okay, says Tonio. Rum is good. Do you have Coke? No, says Sacha, I have milk and I have juice. Let's have juice, says Rosa. She is lying on Sacha's bed now with her hands behind her head. You are so drunk aren't you Sacha? I'm still pretty drunk, Sacha admits, I've been drinking for days.

The other man, who hasn't said anything until now says, What kind of juice? I thought you said this guy would fix us up. Do you have any weed? Maybe I have a little weed, maybe just a joint, but I don't have much weed, I don't even know if I can find it, says Sacha.

Now Tonio is plugging in the Christmas lights around Sacha's window. Let's have some atmosphere, what do you say Sacha? This place is a shithole, says the other man. What is your name, my name is Sacha, says Sacha to the man he doesn't know. Fuck off, what do you want with my name, cabron? says the man.

Sacha looks closely at the man for the first time. The man has very small eyes in a mean face and he is wearing a tee shirt that says LA Lakers on it. Come on, Charlie, be nice, says Rosa languidly from the bed. Sacha is a friend of Tonio and this makes him a friend of mine. Charlie kicks something on the floor and the dog gives a howl. Fucking dog, says Charlie. Leave the dog alone, Charlie, says Sacha. Find the weed, man, says Charlie, I'm sick of this shit.

I don't know if I can find it, says Sacha. Maybe it's under your pillow, says Rosa, and she rolls over on the bed and the vest rides up her back and Sacha notices the flesh above her belt and how smooth it is, and the smooth backs of her legs. He is still so drunk and on top of being drunk, tired, and he cannot stop staring at Rosa, her skin is like the ocean in his dreams with orange glints of light and when he is thinking this he is simultaneously having a fantasy of what it would be like to have Rosa in his bed without her clothes on and how he would like to touch her dark nipples and the flesh on her back, which is when Charlie knocks him on the side of his head with something hard like a rock, it can't be his hand, and he falls over, which is when Tonio says, Take it easy Charlie, slow down man.

Sacha is on the floor with his eyes closed and the dog of Sacha is licking his face. Fucking dog, says Charlie, the guy was lusting after Rosa, that's why, I saw the way the son of a bitch looked at her, man, don't tell me take it easy, man, cabron. And Rosa from her place on the bed, still languid, starts to laugh and says she thinks she found the weed in Sacha's pillowcase and sure enough she is holding up what looks like a joint.

Is she your girlfriend? asks Sacha from the floor. His eyes are opened now and he is thinking that if Rosa is Charlie's girlfriend he can understand why he hit him with whatever it was. But Tonio says, No man, Rosa is Charlie's sister. Oh well then, says Sacha, because he can understand that too, and he says, Look man, to Charlie, but Charlie is on the bed lighting up the joint with Rosa and Sacha can hear the hissing sound of the joint being inhaled and held in the lungs and then the hissing sound of the smoke being exhaled.

Sacha, why don't you get up from the floor and have some of this weed? says Rosa. She is laughing because she can see that Sacha is too drunk and hurt to get up and it suddenly strikes her funny that he is on the floor with a certain look on his face of resignation. Sacha, she says, up, up! And she is laughing so hard she starts to cough. Charlie is quiet now and he is taking many hits of a joint and inhaling and exhaling very fast and when the joint is down to a roach he says in a deep growling voice, a muffled voice buried under the weight of marijuana, Sacha is a dead man.

There is at that point a stunned silence in the room, even Rosa stops laughing and looks nervously at Tonio who is sitting over by the window drinking rum and has been especially quiet all this time but now he finds his voice. What do you mean, man, what're you talking about?

This weed is shit, says Charlie by way of explanation, I think it's poisoned, I feel like shit, I bet it's laced with PCP or some shit. No, Charlie, how could it be laced with PCP? Nobody laces with PCP anymore, Charlie, you know that. This fucker's been tampering with the fucking pot and I'm going to fucking kill him, says Charlie. No, says Rosa finally, Charlie, don't be crazy, sit down over by me Charlie, relax and take it easy, because Charlie is now standing over Sacha and Sacha sees his little eyes in his mean face, eyes that are so small they are inscrutable really in a face which is actually a fat face with little pockmarks on the cheeks and large nostrils. Sacha looks briefly into the nostrils and they are dark inside and he can see the little hairs in the nostrils quiver and he closes his eyes. How stupid to notice someone's nostrils right before death, he is thinking.

Meanwhile the dog has decided to howl. It goes over by the window, by Tonio, and starts in, it throws its head back and lets out the howling sound, and Rosa is delighted by this. How adorable! she says, listen to the adorable dog! What's the dog's name Sacha? And Sacha opens his eyes and there are Charlie's nostrils in the same place but Charlie himself seems to have fazed out slightly, his eyes are a little out of focus and he seems not to be paying attention anymore, even though he continues to stand over Sacha in a menacing way.

The dog's name? says Sacha, and he frowns to himself because it doesn't occur to him until this minute that the dog might require a name, the dog who has been his faithful friend, who has stuck by him, even now the dog is probably howling to save his, Sacha's life. I don't know its name, says Sacha finally.

You don't know its name? says Rosa in disbelief. You don't know its name? she says again. How long have you had the dog? I don't know how long, says Sacha, maybe three or four years. Male or female? says Rosa. What? says Sacha, because this is another thing that Sacha has no idea about.

The truth is he never had any curiosity about the gender of the dog until this minute and he closes his eyes again and tries to remember the dog in various contexts and tries to recall if he ever noticed balls or a penis on the dog and since he couldn't call forth an image of this sort, he says to Rosa, I think it's a girl.

What do you mean you think? You don't know if this dog that you've had for three or four years is a girl or boy? It's a girl, says Sacha, I'm sure of it. But then he thinks that if it were a girl it would have had babies by now and Sacha knows for a fact that the dog hasn't had any babies. There's only one way to settle it, says Rosa, and she rises from the bed and tugs a bit at her vest which has this time begun to ride up in the front, though Sacha doesn't see since he is still on the floor between the legs of Charlie who continues to look down on him in an out-of-focus way.

Then Rosa is going over to the dog who all this time has been howling at various pitches and she grabs its forearms and tries to turn it over. Leave the dog alone, please, says Sacha, because now there are a series of hard little yelps which Sacha never heard coming from the dog. What's up? says Charlie. What's up with the dog? And he steps over Sacha and goes to where Rosa is trying to turn the dog over.

Need some help, Baby? he says to Rosa who is struggling with the resisting dog, kneeling on one of its legs and trying to wrestle it onto its back. Then Charlie's hand goes up and there's something in it, Sacha from his position on the floor can't see quite what it is, and he shouts, No! and at the same time Tonio tries to grab Charlie's hand but it is too late. The hand with whatever is in it crashes on the dog's rib cage and the dog gives a long shudder and Rosa screams, What the fuck Charlie, you fucker! And she beats him with her hands and Tonio says, We better get going.

He walks over to where Sacha is still lying on the floor, this time with his hands covering his eyes, and says, Sorry man, and then Sacha hears the door opening in back of Rosa's terrible screaming. Rosa must be the last to go, and she must still be hitting Charlie because behind her screams Sacha hears the soft thudding of her fists on his shoulders.

Then the door closes and it is silent, except for a thin noise coming from the dog and Sacha rises uneasily to his knees and crawls to where the dog lies with its eyes closed, taking deep breaths of air and shuddering uncontrollably in between and making that thin noise.

The dog is dying, thinks Sacha, and there is nothing I can do about it. What can I do about it? he says out loud to the dying dog. And the dog is in too much pain to have a corresponding thought.

I'm sorry, says Sacha finally, and he puts his hand on the dog's face. Until this minute he never noticed what a valiant jaw the dog has, even though now it is clamped tightly in pain. Sacha pulls himself to his feet and runs the tap water in the sink. Then he takes out a saucer and fills it and, without bothering to turn off the top, he puts the bowl over by the dog's head. He goes to his own bed and rips off the blanket and covers the dog with the blanket, wrapping the blanket more or less around the shuddering dog only not too tightly because he can see it is injured in its chest. Then he kneels on the floor next to the dog and listens to the little breaths of the dog coming faster and then slower, and the thin noise fading out and then coming on again.

And so it goes deep into the night with the dog breathing and the water running into the sink, and after a while Sacha doesn't know if it's the water or the dog he's hearing. It seems to him he hears the dog in the sound of the water and the water in the sound of the dog, and eventually he drifts off to sleep with his head next to where the dog is breathing its last breaths and he continues his dream about the ocean.

ECLIPSE

CHRISTINA HAS AN INTEREST in watercolors. Not the complex contemporary ones whose purpose it is to disguise the medium, whose texture is more like thick oil paint or like metal or glass, overly smooth, with the colors blended too exactly. No, the kind of painting Christina admires has the fresh spontaneous look, the watercolors of Winslow Homer, for example, the vibrant almost luminous colors of the sea and the waves and the rough texture of the paper upon which the wet color is allowed to eddy into little dark tributaries or melt into paler liquid fields, causing those lucky accidents artists pray for.

Christina would like to be a competent watercolorist, she has no interest in being famous, but she would like to be able to achieve a series of seascapes with moody skies and egg-shaped drifting clouds or a series of mountain scenes with little paths or rivers or peaks streaked with purple and green.

She comes here to learn the art of watercolor, therefore, and because it is summer her mother, who has been given a two-week vacation from her job as a marketing consultant in Stuttgart, decides to accompany her. But this city for Christina, right off the bat, is a disappointment. First there are the exorbitant prices of the classes at the art school which she had not anticipated. Then there is the Maestro, Señor Robert Flores, a balding man with ears that stick out and hair that grows out of the lobes, who aside from this deplorable appearance has a droning voice and nothing very interesting to say.

If you want a lighter shade, he instructs, for example, make it more watery. I am not a moron, says Christina under her breath in German. Christina is insulted by this kind of instruction and further is insulted by the class itself which is full of middle-aged American women with dyed hair and overbearing mannerisms.

In addition, this city is supposed to be famous for a wild nightlife. Well. A few discos with pathetic bands, most of whom are lip syncing, if you call that wild. In a place called Lefty's a black man actually sings the blues, but he is off key; moreover, it is a wretched little place, full of short noisy men and women with stinky hairspray. Christina almost gags on her beer, and for a moment she feels horribly trapped while at the same time a sickening feeling of alienation washes over her, as though there is destined to be no place in the entire world where she'll feel comfortable, ever, and she finds herself wishing there were someone to hold her in case she faints from terror; and although she is acquainted with a few people in the club—a lesbian couple, a large American man who plays the guitar, an Australian woman called Pauline—she casts about for a more miraculous salvation, the handsome, intelligent, and sensitive stranger, who in her heart of hearts she knows will never come.

That night she takes a taxi home by herself, despite the warnings that several foreign women have recently been pistol whipped by cab drivers and robbed. When she arrives home her mother, Anka, is scrubbing laundry in the kitchen sink. Anka has her usual long-suffering air, but this does not prevent her from giving a little knowing chuckle when Christina collapses on the sofa with a groan.

Don't worry, at least you'll have clean clothes tomorrow, Anka says. Christina wishes she'd remembered how annoying her mother could be when she suggested this visit to Mexico, but somehow she always manages to forget that sad fact. Away from her mother for a few months, her memory becomes bathed in an unrealistic glow and then she imagines she misses her mother desperately. By dint of some mysterious mental operation, she is able to blot out all of Anka's negative characteristics and filter through only the bearable ones: her nice smell before bed, her industry, and her sympathetic nature, all of which in real life irritate Christina immensely.

What she most forgets is her mother's colossal vanity. After she wrings out the last of Christina's underpants and drapes them over the kitchen chair to dry, Anka goes to the mirror next to the stairs and fusses with her hair. Before she left Stuttgart she had gotten an unfortunate haircut and as a result one piece of hair sticks up from the crown. Anka is constantly checking on this piece of hair, plastering it down with a spray bottle of water and gel, and now in the mirror next to the stairs she fluffs her hair over her ears and turns her head left and right.

How about this style, Christina, do you think it's a bit more youthful? This is the kind of remark that makes Christina want to wring her mother's neck. Instead she doesn't respond at all.

But Anka, for all her vanity and guilt mongering, has a valiant side. Observe her drawing on eyeliner, even though the pencil skids across the aging eyelid leaving clots of black, just one more of the indignities of life, as she is liable to remark to Christina. And now mascara, which does nothing really to enhance the eye but rather calls attention to the deep circles beneath and the crow's feet.

Soon, however, despite the rather lackluster time they've been spending together, there is a happy development in their lives. Which is that an exceedingly good looking man is passing through town and naturally shows an interest in Christina. They first spot him at a restaurant with his family, his mother and perhaps his younger sisters, though you'd never know, one might be his lover. The man has deep set blue eyes and black hair and reminds both Anka and Christina of a young Daniel Day Lewis.

The restaurant is very dim, situated in a courtyard with candles flickering on each table and so it is not possible to absolutely verify the man's similarity to Daniel Day Lewis, but Christina catches the man's eye and smiles and he smiles back and Anka says, He's looking at you again, and Christina lowers her eyes to her steak au poivre and says, Good. These, in fact, are the most interesting moments Christina and her mother have spent since they came to town.

————

Later Christina and the man meet. His name is Sabo which, as she remarks later to Anka, is a stupid name, but he makes good eye contact which impresses her and he is indeed very handsome. He is an artist himself, a creator of installations, an art form Christina has always found a bit pointless, but there you are. They are standing at the entrance to the restaurant chatting the way you do when you meet an attractive person. Christina finds herself smiling more than usual, the corners of her lips curving up, and her whole body seeming to relax and loosen in his presence.

Still, what she is saying is strangely at odds with her body language. Let's face it, she says touching his wrist briefly, this is a dreary place. I had expected so much more. Sabo grins in a droll way. I never would have said dreary. I find it charming and full of character. And the people are wonderful, so warm. Oh please Sabo, says Christina, can't you see they are all assholes? Sabo is amused. You think so? I don't really see that at all. But you can tell he is admiring her good figure through her orange silk dress and his smile is indulgent. Let's walk somewhere, he suggests.

She takes his arm as they walk, first down Hernandez Macias and then up the log road to Dolores Hidalgo. They glide gracefully over the cobbles, in the way of beautiful people, without turning their ankles or stumbling the way the rest of us do, and Christina imagines what an incongruous picture they must make in this setting with their sophisticated conversation and their urban glamour.

She is telling him about her watercolor class. Horrible! she says. And these people are so passionate about their mediocre little paintings, you'd think they were Picasso. What are you passionate about? asks Sabo, and Christina laughs in a knowing way because she understands this question as provocative, an ouverture sexuelle.

Seriously, says Sabo, what do you paint? Oh who knows? says Christina. A disconsolate quality creeps into her voice and she unhitches herself from Sabo's arm. I hate all this fuss about art, she says suddenly. It's not as if it really means something. Sabo laughs hard at this, as if Christina had just told a great joke, but his laughter fades as he looks at the façade of a building with its centuries old stone, purple and gold in the moonlight, and at the moon itself which glances off everything, the windows with their wrought iron grill work, the cobbles, and especially Christina's hair with its salmon-colored shine.

Well? he says. He passes his hand over the top of her head and down the length of her hair, and this assures her of his romantic intentions.

They agree to meet the next day in El Jardin. Don't be late, says Christina, I hate to be kept waiting on those uncomfortable benches. Don't worry, says Sabo and when he kisses her chastely on the forehead, she feels a throb of excitement in her throat and she thinks, *Finally*.

————

You looked especially gemütlich, last night, says Anka with pleasure, because it gratifies her to see Christina the object of everyone's

longing—the women out of envy, the men out of lust—as she herself
had been not so many years ago. It gives her a feeling of continuity, a
conviction that her life has significance beyond herself, because what
after all is the purpose of children if not to import in the very filaments
of their DNA the best characteristics of their parents? In this manner,
the boundaries between parent and child break down and, more impor-
tantly, the boundaries of the self—both physical and mental—dissolve
and become meaningless. When Anka is able to see things in this light
she is actually lifted from her petty concerns and only strays occasionally
to the mirror to tend the errant piece of hair and otherwise preen.

Now Christina is getting ready for her date and Anka watches with
pride as her lovely daughter steps into a pair of Rag & Bone jeans and
arranges a white linen shirt over a silky tank. Or should I wear the black
tee? she asks her mother. Hmmm, says Anka with serious reflection, the
trouble with the tee is it looks hot. On the other hand, it shows off your
waistline.

—But the linen looks breezy.

—More classical.

—But Sabo perhaps is not so classical.

—An artist, this is true. How about the white jeans and the blue chiffon
with your lacy teddy beneath?

—I'll try it.

And so on. She finds herself unusually anxious in anticipation of her
date with Sabo. Something about the feeling of his lips on her forehead,
it went right through her like an electric shock. And then there was the
way she knew they looked together: Perfect. She hadn't realized until now
how lonely she'd been, and though Sabo was not exactly a like-minded
spirit, his resemblance to Daniel Day Lewis and his drollness were enough
to sustain her through the coming weeks, she felt sure.

At last Christina is ready (actually, it doesn't matter what she chooses to
wear—all her clothes are becoming) and she kisses Anka on both cheeks

and Anka waves from the little balcon as if she were a young mother again and Christina a schoolgirl. But when Christina gets to the appointed place, El Jardin in front of the big church, Sabo is not there.

———

Disconsolately, she sits on the stone wall and dangles her feet. Around her a mangy white dog with a spiraled tail hovers. This is a dog she's noticed before, a dog who seems human, not so much a scavenger dog as a dog in search of companionship. A dog who does not sniff Christina but gazes longingly into her eyes with a semblance of understanding.

There are not many people in El Jardin for some reason, and the sky is a strange color, yellowish and murky, and the wind has come up fast and hot, blowing dust onto the lenses of Christina's sunglasses. The dog sits close to Christina's dangling feet with an attitude of respect and when the bells of the big Parroquia strike the fifteen minute mark Christina gives a hiss of irritation and the dog flinches sharply in empathy.

At this point the sky darkens alarmingly and when Christina looks at it she has a sensation of unfamiliarity, as if she's been transported to another planet. The wind is buffeting her sharply and the dog trembles as does Christina's long hair, which whips her cheeks and neck and hurts her. There is hardly anyone left in El Jardin; the man selling balloons that look like soccer balls has taken cover in a doorway, the street vendors with their splattering and hissing taquitos and papas have folded their tables and gone home with their huge iron pans under their arms. Even the shoeshine boys scurry away, screeching joyously in the odd light, twirling their dirty rags above their heads like gloomy flags, the last to leave.

Only Christina remains. And the dog. With the sane part of her, the part that is practical, prudent, and a little paranoid, she tells herself to leave at once. Obviously, she's been stood up. The guy, Slick or Sluggo or whatever his name was, will not come for whatever reason. Perhaps he's dead. But something not quite sane or practical compels her to wait a bit longer.

Through the murkiness and dust and the greyish pallor that seems to have settled ominously over the square, Christina makes out the elaborate spires of the cathedral, the arches of grey stone, the occasional glints of light on the narrow windows, and a mood comes over her, and accompanying it, a notion: that even while the air is weighted and oppressive, every earthly thing in El Jardin—the green metal benches, the glossy, topiaried trees, the stone wall, the dog, and Christina herself—has become incredibly light and insubstantial, as if about to lift into the sky.

She grips the rough stones of the wall and feels the dog knock against her ankles. She imagines herself flying up above everything, like the most delicate and resilient of kites, and this makes her grip the stones more arduously. All the while, the Jardin is becoming murkier, as if a cloud has descended and engulfed the little plaza. The Parroquia has disappeared altogether and only the twitching white ears of the dog are discernible, like little flames. Then she hears her name: Christina. She feels a tap on her shoulder.

The Maestro leans very close. What are you doing out in the eclipse? he asks her. Oh, is that what's going on? she says. I wondered. It's very beautiful, no? says the Maestro. She can smell his breath, he is leaning that close, and with a shudder she feels his hip touch her own as he settles beside her on the wall.

Yes, he repeats, very beautiful the way the world gradually disappears at such times. When the image is gone what have you left? He drones on. Do things cease to exist when we are unable to see them? This is what we'd like to believe. But the world goes on without us, which is a ridiculous fact, almost unthinkable . . .

He pauses for a response from Christina and, as none is forthcoming, he emits a prolonged moan, an excruciatingly intimate sound so full of pain that the white dog leaves its post at the feet of Christina and resituates itself along the shin of the Maestro, leaning tenderly against him as if it had understood every word.

This is when Christina feels a pang of isolation so sharp it takes her breath away. For several minutes, she watches the Maestro and the dog, collapsed into one another in a way that makes her unbearably sad. And as the air lifts in fragile, luminous waves, and color floods El Jardin like a dream, it occurs to her that she doesn't know anything: neither the condition of the sky, nor sorrow or contentment.

Life is full of poorly-timed catastrophes, says the Maestro finally. That's what I love about it. But you are weeping my dear, why are you weeping?

The colors! says Christina.

What about them? asks the Maestro.

I'll miss them! she says, and she covers her face with her hands.

ZACK

I S IN LOVE WITH Jessica. She is very beautiful and everyone, not only Zack, thinks so. She works from nine to two every night in La Cielo, the nightclub that excludes indigenous people and those with beards, and she wears a white shirt and a red tie and an apron. Even in the dim light of La Cielo, the red tie a fat lump at her throat, she is beautiful, she glows like a star, and the customers often forget what they were about to order when she stands in front of them with her notepad. Let's see, how about a Johnny, what was it?, Johnny someone, I can't remember. Johnny Walker on the rocks, says Jessica without smiling. Because like so many people she is weary of this reaction to her beauty and her weariness has made her cold. When Zack comes into the bar, even though he brings her flowers—a bunch of smelly lilies wrapped in their own dusty green leaves and purchased for 10 pesos from a boy who looked about 6—even though he sets the flowers discretely off to the side of the bar, on a low shelf, and asks Horacio to wait until an appropriate moment to offer them to Jessica, while he, Zack, sits off in a more or less darkened corner, at the edge of her station, near the old man with the pink pants and the cowboy boots and the hair growing out of his large earlobes, even though he does all of this in an effort to show his greater sensitivity compared to all others who think only of their own instant gratification in the face of Jessica's stupendous beauty, even though, she ignores him. He sits next to the man whose cowboy boots are crossed at the ankles and who is drinking a Modelo Negra and he considers initiating a conversation because it seems to him the man is as lonely as he is. They sit beneath a mural of a naked woman with her arms raised high and her stomach muscles taut and she is floating in some kind of sea or sky, Zack thinks, while nearby a well-built naked man floats on his side with his penis in a semi-erect state. Zack cannot help but envision the ridiculous picture he and the old man must make sitting beneath this mural and he thinks that if at least they could converse instead of sitting there staring glumly or uneasily into space, the absurdity of the scene would dissipate. But the old man seems lost in his thoughts and Zack cannot think of how to start a conversation. He could say, Lots of people here tonight, or he could comment on the mural, but maybe the man likes the mural, so instead he could say What do you think of the mural or something like that, he could comment on the temperature, like It's too cold in here or too hot in here, but it happens that the temperature in La Cielo is just right, neither too hot or cold and how do you comment on that? Meanwhile, he catches Jessica's eye and she curves the corners of her mouth at him in what is actually a cold and rather perfunctory smile but which Zack takes as encouragement nonetheless. At the sight of Jessica all thoughts of the old man and the mural leave Zack's mind and he can only think of her, Jessica, who looks adorable in her apron and red tie with her hair in long braids tonight and her slender perfect body—far more perfect than the woman depicted on the mural—wending through the crowd bearing a tray of cocktails and ashtrays with incredible grace. Oh Jessica, thinks Zack, the words forming in his mind like the beginnings of a song or a poem. When she disappears from view, behind the bar with its row of noisy customers, it is as though she is still there, her image before his eyes like a dream, every detail of her, the braids, the tie, the apron, the delicate hands bearing the cocktail tray, intact.

Meanwhile the old man has begun to cough painfully into a handkerchief and sounding as if he will choke. It is an alarming and uncontrolled-sounding cough and people from nearby tables have stopped their conversations in order to stare at the man and at Zack who is at this point clapping him on the shoulder in a hapless attempt to bring him around. But the old man, bending over with his head between his knees, his handkerchief pressed alternately to his mouth and eyes, cannot seem to stop; indeed, his cough, which began as a rich and varied baritone rumble is now more of a tenor h-h-hacking, monotone and interminable, and in between, which is to say hardly at all, he gasps for breath and waves away Zack and also Jessica who has arrived with a glass of water. Finally, almost at the exact moment someone from the other side of the room stands up and shouts Heimlich Maneuver! The man stops coughing and wipes his eyes and takes a small sip of the water.

Thank you, he says to Zach in a hoarse voice. And he nods to Jessica as well, who does not seem concerned as much as aggravated by the diversion of the coughing man. Okay then, she says to Zack with a brisk, single nod of her head. That's settled. And she moves into the haze of crowded tables and cigarette smoke. That woman is rather extraordinary looking, says the old man to Zack. His voice is still hoarse from all the coughing, but he is sipping his Modelo Negra and puffing a cigarette as if nothing happened. She has the look, he continues, of a Sistine Madonna, seductive and virginal at once. And those fierce eyes, so angry and ingenious! Here the man sighs loudly and shakes his head, as if, Zack thinks, there were something inevitably ruined about Jessica and those like her, something doomed to a tragic outcome. She is a beautiful woman, Zack agrees. And without meaning to he tells the man, I'm in love with her. Abruptly, the man thrusts out his hand. Robert Flores, Maestro. Zack, says Zack shaking the damp hand. It's a pleasure, says Robert Flores. Salud, he says raising his Modelo. Here's to love and to beautiful women, may they rest in peace, no pun intended. Zack sips his own beer. What's the pun? he asks Robert Flores after a moment. What? says Robert Flores. He is bending over and reaching into his cowboy boot to scratch his ankle. You said No pun intended, says Zack. So I did, says Robert Flores, What was I saying again? Something about beautiful women resting in peace. I see, says Robert Flores. I don't remember. Where did that girl go anyway? I need a beer and a match. Your face and my ass, says Zack, grinning. What's that supposed to mean? says Robert Flores. Oh it's just an expression, an old joke, says Zack. You say it to people who ask for a match. Ah, says Robert Flores, nodding gravely into his Modelo. But it's not funny. People usually think it's funny, says Zack, a little uneasy. No offense, he adds. I see, says Robert Flores. Did you say you were fucking this girl? I didn't say, says Zack. I only said I was in love with her. She's very beautiful, says Robert Flores, I hope for your sake you're fucking her. Only I wish she'd come and bring me a beer. Oye gorgeous, he says snapping his fingers at Jessica who is taking orders from a new table of customers. How about some service? Zack feels himself redden. She'll be here in a minute, he tells Robert Flores, you don't have to shout. Touchy touchy, says Robert Flores, laughing. Hey Zack, you forgive an old man, please. I'm thirsty as hell is all. A beautiful woman exists in the universe like a sculpture or a symphony. She is there to inspire, to lift us to the skies. Here Robert Flores looks at the ceiling of La Cielo and points.

In point of fact, Zack has made love to Jessica once. He is one of the very few, according to his friends. Many have tried but only two or three have been chosen, Gabriel told him. She is particular. And so Zack had felt blessed when, on the night before last, she'd unsmilingly invited him to her house and then to her bed, removing her clothes with the same efficiency and grace she wiped the round metal tables at La Cielo. He, a young man of barely twenty years of age, a gringo with a baseball cap and jeans with a rip at the knee, an overly thin man, whose hands and feet seemed strangely at odds with the rest of his body, proportionately larger and therefore more masculine. Then he had lain next to her, naked, and breathed in her sweet, smoky scent and circled her small breasts with his hands and sucked her tiny hard nipples and the skin of her neck and her earlobes in what he hoped was a practiced and sophisticated manner. In a corner of the room, her cat meowed plaintively and this strange accompaniment, like a love song, was full of longing and sorrow. Afterwards Jessica asked him to leave in the same unsmiling way that she'd invited him home. She reminded him to flip the lock on his way out as she was too tired to get out of the bed.

———

Now she stands in front of Robert Flores with her notepad and her pencil poised for his order. What? is all she says. I want another Modelo and I want to say you are beautiful, though you know this already.

A beer? Chips? Also, turning to Zack, you shouldn't have spent money on those flowers. They are already dead. I'm sorry, says Zack, remembering the small boy, the bony fingers clutching the white gardenia-smelling flowers, and the drunken couple arguing on the street, another beautiful woman, though older, and a short, balding man wearing bright green golf pants with little circles on them. I mean I'm sorry they died, he tells Jessica and he blushes, self-conscious with her standing there, a severe expression on her beautiful face, an expression that makes her face darker and even more beautiful, it seems to him, a subtle complication traversing the perfect features like a wind passing over a lake. De nada. Don't worry about it, she says.

Women, says Robert Flores sympathetically. I couldn't help overhearing. You bring them flowers and they disdain you. Not at all, says Zack. Really. But Robert Flores is clearly not convinced. Men are fools, women are bitches, may they rest in peace. Before Zack can respond, Jessica is setting the Modelo in front of Robert Flores and the old man is grabbing her wrist. I was telling Zack here, he says, that women are bitches, what do you think? Astonishingly, Jessica laughs. I think you're right señor, she says. And men are fools. That's just what I said, didn't I, Zack? You did, sir, those were your exact words. Not one minute ago I said the same thing, repeats Robert Flores. Amazing. But Jessica is already on her way, the two men watch the cha-cha-cha of her nice ass swinging

If I could o-o-only wake up to you Baby
in the cold morning light
put my shoes in front of me Baby

Scooping up the empties, bottles, glasses, and the remains, lime rinds, cigarette butts, eyes straight ahead, unflinching in the cool lake of her face, into which the yearning yearning yearning tumbles and drowns—

Oh Jessica.

———

Magda had never seen Zack nor had Zack seen Magda. She is high again, a snootful, coke and pot, a little vodka, it's okay, she's okay.

At La Cielo, heaven of tombs, its grainy mirrored surfaces. That mural of heaven itself, naked bodies afloat. But at the moment all bodies collide, boundary-less. She herself with a boy who looks exactly like James Dean, she tells him. Ma'am? he says. This is Zack on his way to the men's room. Looking into her weary out-of-focus eyes. Lovely, she is saying. Mine are green.

She wears a sweater. Green as the moon would turn. She once had green eyes, a man said, and so for that moment she had them. Like a cat's, looking into the man's. Saw herself looking; through his eyes. This phenomenon only a woman's. Looking outside and through another to the inside of which one is.

Otherwise, the shape of a zero. N-n-nothing. C-c-catastrophic.

She wants wings but who doesn't?

Meanwhile, Billie singing:

> *If the moon turns green*
> *And shadows get up and walk around*
> *Clouds come tumbling to the ground:*
> *I wouldn't be surprised*

and La Cielo holding its tricky mood of shadows, of impending accidental encounters, light too hard on a girl's throat, her own. Glistening and attractive. High as a kite. As the green moon, rather or instead. A state of being that permits these clarifying intersections. The green moon, the green thought. Rivers on the back of the hand and aging tributaries. Light snuffed from the eye. Beautiful waitress's high heel shoes on the concrete, clop-clop, beating out time and space.

What time is it?

On his way out, Zack smiles, in all sincerity, the woman looks bad, screwed up. Do you want a drink? he asks. It's the nicest thing a person has said in years, *do you want a drink*, offering to treat and serve, kind of a zenith in this era of the life. Would Elvira have said it? Would she, before bed, before the many many ablutions of Elvira, teeth and scrubbing and cream and lather, slipping arms from the flowered bra straps, breasts innocent, as if unused, reflecting a twin cute glare. Would she have thought of this simple, human need for a drink on the part of her friend, her sometimes, one time at least, lover, Magda, would she? Nada. Nunco.

Now the boy, James Dean, hair short at the sides with the exact top flip and sideburns as in "East of Eden," takes her arm, propels her to a round table, a round seat, an unconscionable looking companion, wild-eyed, large-eared, hirsute. Robert Flores, he tells her without being asked. Flores, she says, because of all this, it's the best word in the mouth, like absinthe or fellatio. *'Cause anything can happen*, sings Billie on the record and Magda is compelled to repeat the sentiment to Flores, who has taken her hand, is smoothing the knuckled veins on the back of it. And this, he tells James Dean, is what finally happens to them all. Heartbreak. Magda feels his hand slide to her neck, one finger grazing her cheek. Terrible terrible. What's so terrible? says Magda. Because I'm a little fucked up? I'm not that fucked up. You think I'm a whore?

We shouldn't talk about her as if she's not here, says Zack. Then Jessica comes with a coaster, a beer for Magda. Compliments of Zack, says Jessica. Who the fuck is Zack? says Magda. James Dean? This guy? You know, she tells Jessica, leaning close, showing her long yellow teeth in a smile, he fucked me last night. It's the truth. When Magda laughs, Zack can see down her throat to darkness, the nubbin of that thing, whatever they call it, shaking like a miniscule red lightbulb. Jessica says to Zack, We should get her home. We can't afford trouble here. Zack asks Magda, where do you live?

Fuck off, all of you, says Magda. Jesus. When she stands the lights descend and spin. My heart's an open book, she says, staggering away. She knows this; feels the stagger in her gait and head, the ch-ch-chunk of skin and brains coming up the runway. Then she falls. Smack. A sound like melons on the freeway, the zero of nothing and then the din of those surrounding, James Dean and the glorious braided woman and the Maestro with earlobe hair. Others like phantom mountains, a jagged blur in the dark, blood-laden scape.

It's everywhere, Magda's blood. People are slipping on it. It's sticking to clothing and skin. Call an ambulance.

———

Zack is the one who holds Magda, who presses the striped towel to her wound, cradling her head. She has fallen backwards, she has cracked open the back of her skull. Bone on slate, the sound had been terrible. He hated pain and now he was face to face with it. Pain in a green sweater. Ribbons of blood wending their careless ways. A trickle caresses his shoe. It makes him feel he is choking.

What he can't get over is his own proximity. Here in his hand, the head of Magda, bleeding. The eyes of Magda flickering, open then closed, then open again. I don't want a fucking ambulance. She hisses this. Get me a drink, she hisses. Vodka.

And here is Jessica, exchanging the blood-soaked towel for a clean one. And Robert Flores who grabs his sleeve. A beautiful woman, he is saying, or has he already said this? Not now, señor, says Zack, trying to be respectful, but Robert Flores says, she was once beautiful, you can read the signs. Observe the curve of the jaw, the cheekbones. The arched, haughty quality traversing the forehead. The mark of a beautiful woman is not easily diminished

Oh please old man, says Jessica. Sit down, she says. Everyone, she says, because now people have begun to gather, whispering and some even laughing. Go back to your tables.

When Zack observes his own hand, he sees it is trembling. But whether it is trembling from the spectacle of Magda's blood which covers his own like water from a tap, or whether it is because Jessica is so close, the heat of her sweet arm next to his, the smoky scent of her skin, he doesn't know.

There is a lot of commotion as if everyone were being industrious and helpful. The gossip that surrounds such incidents has already begun to take shape. Who is the woman who fell? She is a visiting dignitary from Bolivia. She has been slipped a mickey at Pancho's. She is a drug dealer from Texas. She is a lesbian. Etc. Etc.

When the ambulance comes it's no different. It is hushed at first, in order to hear the various transactions between the medics and the patient, but then the chatter accelerates and amplifies. The patient is saying, No fucking way, assholes. And Zack is saying, You have to take her anyway, to the medics, who are saying We can't take her if she doesn't want to go. Anyway, it's just a superficial head wound. But there's blood everywhere, Jessica is saying. It's not superficial, she has the gash the size of a fist. Cabrone, leave me alone, Magda is saying, shut up. Chinga, I got blood all over my fucking shirt, someone else is saying. Es una loca. And Robert Flores is saying, Everything comes down to these moments which in their purity and perfection demand our attention.

When the ambulance leaves, Zack is holding the hand of Magda who has refused medical assistance, who has shut her eyes and begun to hum softly to herself. It makes Zack shiver to look at her. On one eyelid is a little freckle and the green sweater is missing a button. Where is that drink you promised me, James Dean? she asks him, opening one eye. She gives a lopsided grin. Maybe you shouldn't drink at this point, he says. He would like to soothe her, but what can he say? Maybe you should go home.

Then Jessica is standing there. She has changed out of the apron and the red tie and is now wearing a blue, silky dress with little gold spangles on it and high heels. Just seeing her there makes Zack feel better. We should take her in a taxi, she tells Zack. Home is where the heart is, says Magda. That's a laugh.

Zack is not sure why Robert Flores is along for the ride in the taxi. I would be honored to be of assistance, he had told Jessica and Jessica had given him one of her impatient shrugs. In the taxi he says, I am writing a book about such incidents. Crisis, he says, is fascinating. At such moments the world is luminous. Can you feel it?

Who is this guy anyway? A philosopher? The taxi driver, Angelo, is unhappy about taking a bloodied woman in his cab, staining his new leopard seat covers. Ay Jessica, he says. He has known her for years and were it not for the fact that she is beautiful, an angel herself, he would refuse the fare out of practicality. He will now have to change the seat covers or live with the blood stains, red on black and yellow. This will be bad for business, whichever way you look at it. Where does she live? he asks Jessica. Where do you live? asks Jessica. Tell us where you live, repeats Zack, shaking Magda on the shoulder because she is falling asleep and Zack heard somewhere that it's bad to fall asleep with a head wound.

———

Magda feels the spin and grind of another world closing over her. Chinks of light shot into the darkness and she watches, transfixed. I have no idea, a voice not hers, not hers certainly, answers. Because where is Elvira? She may have left her voice with Elvira. In a drawer or under the mattress.

This newer world has more clarity. Black and white. A little memory is wagging across her line of vision, a slip of a memory that has the odor of roses. She sees a vase of them on a pink table, a group of milagros on a chain, arms and legs and hearts. Then someone, a woman, is brushing her long hair. But my hair isn't long anymore, she explains. Once it used to be but E cut it and it fell on the floor. Dead. My hair died, she says. Ha ha, she says. On the movie screen window the night is whirring by and James Dean with his exact *East of Eden* flip is whispering something. Speak up! she says. She believes tears are in her eyes, waiting to fall. Speak up James Dean! she says.

But who was it that brushed her hair? A silver hairbrush. A row of glass perfume bottles. The white curtain wafted in.

Now a man comes with an umbrella. Face of a hammer. Making her head hurt. Pounding in a nail. The hairbrush is dropped and voices like sparrows or like food frying, numerous, complicated voices, like the weavings on the white curtains which waft.

But attend attend attend to the beautiful woman with long dark braids, smoothing her knuckled veins. Through everything, the whirring by darkness and the radio of her memories, she hears this one particular voice. What is she saying?

———

Jessica is saying, We will have to take you to the hospital, it's better this way, you're ok, Magda. But Jessica doesn't know if Magda's okay and feels a certain guiltiness when she assures her, against all reason, that she is. Also, what does it mean to be ok? Is she, Jessica, ok? No, she would have to say she is not.

She is thinking of her cat, Flaca. Flaca is ok, she thinks suddenly. She accepts life for what it is. She is happy anywhere, at the neighbor's or anywhere. She would be happy with the garbage man, thinks Jessica, smiling a little to herself because she pictures the garbage men who are always so cheerful, and Flaca rushing to meet the truck and the man who makes the clanging sound by banging a little rod on an iron bar is the happiest of all. Oye Flaca, he says each morning, do you want to come with me? And Flaca would go, Jessica is sure of it, if Jessica didn't scoop her up under the belly and fling her over the threshold and close the door.

Now there is Zack. Is he ok? She slides her eyes sideways to watch him holding the woman, Magda, touching her hair now with his big hand, smoothing it much in the same way he smoothed her, Jessica's own hair, a few nights ago when she was foolish enough to invite him home. And now he spends his money on flowers that are half dead and gives her those puppy dog looks that can only mean one thing. No, Zack is not ok. Maybe human beings are never ok. Maybe it is a condition of human-ness, to be a little out of sorts even in the best of times.

When Magda moans, Jessica feels guilty for the drift of her thoughts, for not attending carefully to the wounded woman who is half on her lap and half on Zack's in the back seat of Angelo's car, bleeding on the zebra seat cover. What is it? says Jessica. What? What? Do you suppose she's conscious? she asks Zack. And Robert Flores, from his place in the front seat, says, Take her pulse.

They are on their way to the hospital and Jessica is trying to find Magda's pulse in the celery stalk of her wrist and suddenly Angelo announces that he can't remember exactly where the hospital is. Before I had a more or less idea, he says, but now I think I was wrong. They are on a dark street with trees and under the trees some empty cans and old papers glow in the light of the moon. He stops the car and turns on the overhead. Do you have a map? asks Zack. No, he says, I was hoping you do. Because now we are lost, lo siento, I'm sorry. But maybe I can still find it.

See? says Robert Flores. I sensed this would be a calamity, this night, didn't I say that to you, Zack, in the bar? But Zack can't remember Robert Flores saying this and he is searching his memory when Magda says, very clearly, there is no mistaking this word in Magda's mouth, *Flores*. What did I tell you? says Robert Flores. It is fated to be this way.

Oye Flores, shut up now, says Jessica. She is getting aggravated at this old man, who right from the start promised to be an annoyance and now he is proving himself. Angelo, she says, find the hospital. Just find it! Because this is an impossible situation if there ever was one. She is bleeding bad all over the car.

Angelo speeds up the taxi, because he is thinking, truth be told, of the new seat covers and of business, why not admit it, business is important, is his life after all. And then Robert Flores has gone into a fit of coughing again, wiping his eyes and nose with his handkerchief and Angelo says, What did I do to deserve this, Dios Mio? There is nothing to do but drive faster. He barrels down a long hill, the cab lurching and pitching over the uneven pavement, and he rounds a corner, tires squealing like goats, and then he is suddenly in familiar territory. Just beyond the trees and the little shacks of los pobres, he sees the tienda of his cousin Maria Dolores. Thank God. It could be that Maria Dolores has always been good with directions, he thinks he remembers his mother saying this once. So he pulls to a sharp stop, which he knows is sharp and sudden because all the people in the back seat (all except the sick woman) cry out Oh! And Robert Flores pitches forward and hits his chin on the dashboard and immediately stops coughing. This is the tienda of Maria Dolores, he says to his passengers. I will go now for assistance, and he shuts the door of the cab without bothering to wait for a response.

The tienda is dark, which only means it is no longer open to the public, but around back he sees a dim light behind the curtains which means that Maria Dolores, thank goodness, is still up. He raps on her window and then on the door. But no one comes. Maria Dolores! he calls out. It's an emergency! But still no one comes to the door. Then behind him he hears footsteps, a crunching in the dirt and pebbles of the yard, and when he turns he recognizes his cousin Jose Luis who is drunk and weaving unsteadily toward him, holding a bottle of rum close to his heart.

Angelo, says Jose Luis, never have I been so glad to see anyone in my life! Have a drink. No, I can't drink with you tonight, Jose Luis, says Angelo, and he begins to explain the complicated series of events but midway through he realizes the futility of this. I know where the hospital is, says Jose Luis. You better let me come. Ay, Jose Luis, you are so drunk, can't you just explain the directions to me? I don't think so, says Jose Luis. But I know it if I see it and I have a nose I usually follow which is quite good. Shit, says Angelo. You better come. Don't worry, says Jose Luis. Drunk as I am, I'm not stupid. But Angelo crosses his fingers anyway and says a quick petition to the Virgin of Guadalupe, that she will let him reach the hospital in the next 5 or 10 minutes in exchange for which he will not smoke mota for a month.

This is how Jose Luis comes to be crammed in the taxi along with Robert Flores, Zack, Jessica, and Magda who is on her last legs, Angelo says, looking briefly at her face which seems to be shrinking. The new passenger sits on Robert Flores' lap and Robert Flores cannot stop complaining about it. Move your elbow, if you please. Your butt is one of the hardest in creation. I can't breathe. And so on. And Jose Luis lets out a loud unfragrant belch and claps Robert Flores on the back, What did you say this son of a bitch's name was?

Zack cannot remember when it was exactly that he looked into the face of Magda and realized she was dead. He had been listening to the complaints of Robert Flores and to the rantings of Jose Luis and he had been thinking of Jessica, her arm so close to his as they held Magda that, at some point, he found his fingers covering her cool thin ones and he held her hand briefly. He had been thinking, the thought only half-formed, unrealistic, that if only he could be with Jessica forever he would be happy. But, at the same time, he couldn't imagine how this happiness would shape itself; he couldn't imagine any details of their future lives together beyond night after night spent holding her and sighing into her neck. Then he looked at Magda seemingly asleep on his lap, and he realized she was dead.

They had been driving at a breakneck speed and when he informed the others and Robert Flores had instructed him to take the pulse and there was none and when Jessica admitted that the body on her lap had indeed seemed to grow a bit stiff, Angelo slowed down. Chinga, she is dead, yes no? It's a pity, says Angelo. We did what we could, nobody would say otherwise, and though he felt a secret relief that he didn't have to give up mota for a whole month, he was nonetheless truly sorry that the woman died, especially in his taxi. And then for a while, everyone stopped talking. Even Robert Flores and Jose Luis stopped their arguing and it grew very quiet in the car so that all that could be heard was the sound of the tires grinding over the cobblestone streets. Whereas before the atmosphere in the car had been excited and hopeful, there was now, it seemed to Zach, a general gloominess in the air because nobody wanted to be in a car with a corpse.

Then Angelo said Chinga, and began to whistle. And Zack watched the flickering light on the old buildings, the darkness coming and lifting as they rounded a corner, then up the long hill of Santo Domingo. I take you somewhere, says Angelo. Jessica, I take you and the others somewhere special.

But Jessica is thinking of death, of the woman in her green sweater with the missing button and the freckle on her eyelid. Not an hour ago she existed in the world, the same as anyone, breathing and swearing. She had gripped Jessica's hand, she had wept against her apron. She had been a pain in the ass, a bitch, like anyone.

Then they are at the top of the city, on a hillcrest, Angelo swinging the taxi around and under some tall cottonwoods and a crumbling brick building, and he turns off the ignition and opens the door. Come out, he gestures. Follow me. Jose Luis is the first to stumble from his side of the car, still holding his bottle of rum, and Robert Flores comes next. Jessica and Zack take longer, having to first disentangle themselves from the corpse, Magda, resting her top half and then her lower half carefully on the leopard seat cover. And Robert Flores says, Are we going to leave her here alone? referring to the corpse, and Angelo says, She's not going anywhere, let's face it. And Jose Luis says, To be safe, maybe we should stash her in the trunk. But Zack says, No, I don't think we ought to put her in the trunk. Also, I have tires in the trunk, says Angelo. And that settles it.

In the moonlight Zack notices a smear of blood on the front of Jessica's blue dress and on his sleeve, the same color as the pitted footholds they climb to reach the building's flat roof and of the brick building itself, and the orange haze of the city way below, and the warm light on Jessica's hair. And this makes him wonder if everything is connected in some way, a way we have no knowledge of, and if this is the secret of the world.

Over the rooftop, the tall cottonwoods are rustling and hissing, the stars are so clear in the night sky they look like cutlery, knives and forks and spoons. I always think it's very peaceful here, says Angelo, lighting a joint and passing it to Zack. Below, way below, the city in its orange haze, the blackness enfolding the orange, seems to float, as if it's on its way somewhere. Take some, Amigo, and pass it to Jessica, says Angelo. And Zack is thinking, I love Jessica, and it occurs to him to say it, I love you, Jessica, and he hands her the joint.

Meanwhile, over the side of the roof Jose Luis is taking a long piss, but nobody seems to mind. Not even Robert Flores who is gazing at the stars and pointing out constellations: the Big Dipper, Orion, the Pleiades with its seven little sisters. Nothing lasts forever, he is saying, even those little sisters which, as you know, are already dead.

Then across their line of vision, cutting across like the flash of a whip, the unmistakable shape of an empty Modelo bottle, tossed as if by someone hiding in the bushes, and smashing against a rock. But since there is no one in the bushes, they agree this must have been Magda who, traveling at a great rate out of this world, decided to return for an instant and leave some mark on it, the mark that only a ghost can leave and which is therefore indelible.

And Zack is thinking that in this way time passes, at a distance and then close up and then at a distance again. Like waves. And that everything changes and then goes back to where it was. This is why when he puts his arm around Jessica he is hopeful that the moment will return: her heavy braids on his blood-smeared sleeve, and the marijuana smoke bitter in his lungs, and Angelo saying in his rusty voice, She was probably a good woman, yes no? She had a good life. Who's to say?

TURISTA

TODAY WE ARE ALL throwing up. We wake up feeling a little queasy, as if there's an ocean in our estomagos, then we go back to sleep. We dream we are carrying a baby through the cobblestone streets and the baby's name is Nonny. She has black hair that sits on top of her head like cooked spinach, and a beautiful angelic face. She is so intelligent that when we bring her into the room with a big window she says, Are we allowed to bring the outside inside? A worried look crosses her sweet face. Yes, we say, it is permitted.

Outside, in the frame of the window, a woman is walking around a rusted car. This woman, Elvira, is a ceramicist and the reason she walks around the car is to assess its usefulness to her work, which is to make many small square ceramic tiles and then to shroud unlikely objects with them—cars, sofas, articles of clothing. The result is a mood of softness interspersed with hardness, a drama of opposing tensions, like wrestling in church. Once she blanketed a 1959 Chevrolet, erected it on a forty-foot pillar, and set it in the center of a big city. It thrilled her when the inhabitants complained and, moreover, that they were not able to articulate their uneasiness. She loves this—to be beyond language in this way, just slightly out of reach, ineffable. Now she circles the car with her slow stride while behind her the sky is stained a copper color—it must be early morning—which enhances the spectacle of the car so that it glows like a giant fallen star. Occasionally, she touches the car and the gesture, we notice, is tentative, as if she were touching a lover's back for the first time. Otherwise she walks with a measured pace, her hands thrust deep into the pockets of a green felt coat.

Last night, at dinner, someone mentioned this car, abandoned and rusting in a certain neighborhood, and she became immediately interested. She jotted down the address on a napkin, but even as she wrote she felt her enthusiasm waning—it was so far to go and who knew if the car would suit her purposes? And if it did, then there were the complicated arrangements that would have to be made for its transport to her studio. This is how her mind drifted from lively interest to almost total indifference in the space of thirty seconds. She caught the eye of the man who was now reciting the complicated directions, and she smiled, trying to look grateful. She found that he moved something in her, something forgotten or left behind in her life: the way he looked, a young, blond man with a fragile moustache which made him seem younger and raw, and his voice, which was pleasantly soft yet uninflected, almost a monotone.

His effect on her was disturbing and as she rummaged in her mind for the memory—was it a brother or a school friend, what?—she found herself responding to him sexually, her body arching toward him, her hands opening to catch his words. He returned her gaze, boldly stared into her eyes and narrowed his own with a hint of amusement, a quality she found both attractive and challenging. But it was shocking that she should feel such a challenge from one so young, which was when she realized that what she found compelling about him must be that in his very persona, this man held in tentative balance those contradictions that were at the core of her work—softness and hardness, age and youth, authenticity and deceit.

What's wrong with North America, he was saying to her, is that people respond to each other programmatically. There is a distance, forever unmappable, between what people feel and what they say, which means they no longer know how they feel. Permit me to make an analogy. At this, the young man leans towards her and touches her shoulder briefly, for emphasis, she thinks, but she shivers nonetheless. A squirrel eats nuts. In North America there are many nuts but all the squirrels have forgotten how to eat them.

Elvira laughs. What do they do with them then? They horde them, they throw them away, what's the difference? You're a tease, Elvira. And again she feels herself brought up short by this man. Now he is brushing a strand of her hair from her shoulder and soon he will be cupping her face in his one hand while the other will unfasten the buttons of her dress. What can Elvira say about what follows? That she had no will in the proceedings would be stating it both too simply and too emphatically. To say that she was under a spell would be closer to the truth; and to say that in the morning the early sunlight bathed the side of his very young face and lit up the ends of his moustache, the hairs so soft there, they might have been a baby's, and that, because the sheet had slid half down his body, the light fell also on his hairless chest, the chest of a young girl, perhaps, the nipples flat and pink, the skin with its two little moles, little curses, she thought.

This is when she rises soundlessly from his bed and comes to this place, the place of art rather than the place of love, of peace rather than ecstasy. Here she is at home, assessing structural difficulties, watching the glow deepen on a rusted car, the color working itself into the darkest crannies. Instead of the body on the bed, half hidden, asleep, enigmatic, unapproachable. . . .

We watch all this from the window, the outside indeed coming inside, with permission. And Nonny the baby says, When is the end? Because it's dark again and we're walking on the cobblestones toward our mysterious future. Or rather toward a future which embraces and forgets us.

RABBIT IN THE MOON

S HE BEGAN BY PAINTING a landscape in two sections. She used photographs. One was a photo she'd taken of the Rocky Mountains. It had been dark—a cloud descending over a peak. Ocher strips beneath. The other the same mountain, only lighter. She painted the mountains, then ringed them with black, but it was too sectioned off. It didn't make sense, one landscape over another. Purple and green, then gray, then she painted over it, all black.

He came up behind her and touched her waist. It's good, he said. But it wasn't good, it irritated her.

What she wanted was to paint a ballerina, but ballerinas she had painted in the past. Very light and frothy, skipping or floating. She didn't want a floating ballerina. This was not on her mind. She wanted to go forward in her life.

For weeks, nevertheless, she painted the ballerina. One of the students in the class told her it was beautiful. Another said it brought tears to her eyes.

He didn't say anything. He stood behind her and said nothing. He was precise about it. She wanted to be with him but another woman came to call. This woman was stern and beautiful, her hair was a wonderful color of gold. She considered giving the ballerina this color of hair, but she didn't.

She was happy and unhappy, both at once. The other students were painting angels, they used gold leaf. They set up their easels on a balcony overlooking a courtyard, the sculpture garden, the café where people went to write in their journals and read *Atencion*. There was a man there who desired her. She didn't know his name but every day he smiled at her, invited her to sit beside him. She distrusted him.

She painted and painted this ballerina. She gave her square black breasts. Someone liked that. Another one told her to change the legs. The legs pinned the ballerina to the earth and they were awkward, it was true, they were awkward. She didn't want a floating ballerina or even a dancing ballerina. She wanted a ballerina transfixed, weighed down, somehow stunned. A ballerina trapped in the role of ballerina. This is what she had in mind. Nevertheless, she changed the legs. Now they were like wings. They had grace and substance. It's good, he said.

He stood beside her and put his arm around her shoulder. You worry too much, he said. Why do you worry so much? She didn't know how to respond to him. She never knew what to say. She said, I always worry when I'm working, that's just who I am. He walked away.

It was uneasy between them, yet he gave her good advice. Mix some green with the black, he said. When she did, something happened. The ballerina became more complex, distinct.

Then one day, in a master moment, she smeared paint right from the tube over the ballerina's skirt and worked it with her fingers. It was good, she knew it was good, but then the other parts of the painting suffered by comparison.

The other woman continued to visit him. She waited for him on a chair by the window. She flipped through art catalogues. At first she was jealous of the other woman—her gorgeous hair, her sternness—but then she began to admire her. Her legs were firm. Her face was serious and her eyes were unusual—very blue in a tanned, lined face. Her eyes were amazing.

He said to her: Analyze this painting. Look at it for a long time and make decisions. Think about form. Color is something else.

But color was everything to her. And the feel of the paint. It was like food.

But the ballerina suffered. It was static, even in motion, it was static, lifeless, unapproachable. When he approached her, she sighed. She detested the weakness within her that made her sigh. She glanced at the woman flipping through catalogues. It made her happy to see her there and yet she was jealous.

On the last day of class, to her dismay, the ballerina had not improved. Rather, it had become worse. The colors less vibrant, the design stultified. She wanted to burn the canvas. She had no sense of fulfillment.

On the balcony overlooking the courtyard, he and the blonde woman faced each other. He took a cigarette from the pocket of her shirt. She wore interesting clothes, soft leathers and little tunics in greens and blues, sandals on her bony, agile, intelligent feet.

She imagined the woman's feet flexed and pointed under a white sheet, entangled with his.

That last day, the woman brought in a catalogue of her own work to share with the class. The woman was a real painter, it turned out. She used a palette knife and her paintings were strangely muted, simple, emotional. On the back cover was a photograph of the woman sitting in a large white room on a small white couch. It pained her to see this photograph.

She went home and wept and hung the ballerina painting on a wall.

The next day, she scraped it with a palette knife. It was instantly better, all golds and blues and what had been beneath—two landscapes and a ballerina—gave it some texture, dimension. But she couldn't bring herself to entirely efface the ballerina. The ballerina persisted through the layers of paint, as if in a mist. But she liked it better.

Nevertheless, when friends came to visit, they didn't remark much on the painting. One woman said she liked it, but this was someone with poor taste. Someone else said it made her nervous.

After a while it looked dull to her. It wasn't moving. It had no vitality.

She felt the same way. The weather had taken a turn and it was suddenly humid. In the afternoons, it rained. The best part was the way the skies looked before a storm. She was renting a small apartment on the upper story of an old Spanish colonial. From the terrace she watched the gray clouds gather—all shades of gray and black edging out the blue. It was magnificent. Then a few drops would come, then steady rain, thunder and lightning. She went indoors. She looked at the painting and sighed.

She didn't know what she wanted. This was true in her life. She didn't know what she wanted or what she should want or what would be good for her to want. Such vacillation made her weak, she felt.

She made an appointment with a palm reader for the following Tuesday. In the interim, she frequented the bars. Twice she saw him. Once he grasped her shoulder, another time he turned his face away from her.

She wrote him off. Finally, she wrote him off. She didn't care about him anymore. A year ago they had been lovers and now he wouldn't look at her. Her feelings, she discovered, were deeply hurt. She refused to think about him.

They had been lovers and then she had taken a class from him. It had been a mistake. She thought of the woman with the remarkable blue eyes, the great and probably famous painter. How could she compete?

She did other things. She became involved, briefly, with a woman. She slept with her and she found the woman's body too hot, she radiated heat throughout the night and made her uncomfortable. Also, on account of the rain, there were mosquitos.

She plugged in the Mosquifine and got a terrific headache. For three days she took aspirin. She hated the mosquitos and the woman, her lover, was not sympathetic. She decided, finally, that she was hopelessly heterosexual. She told this to the woman, in those words. The woman, her lover, wept.

Finally it was time to go to the palmist, Pamela. Pamela had been an international Vogue model until she gained weight. She had been everywhere, Paris, Rome, Egypt. Her bones were exceptionally fine, her eyes were brown, expertly lined and shadowed. It struck her as strange, though, that her hair was greasy and her clothes were unbecoming and dowdy.

The palmist said, You must learn to let go emotionally. Isn't it true that you withhold something of yourself? She told her to unplug the Mosquifine and wait patiently for a great love to come into her life. She called her hon. Am I right, hon? she said. Or: Write that down, hon, so you won't forget.

After the experience with the palmist, she went home and studied the ballerina painting. Once again, it had become unbearably irritating to her. The palette knife strokes were monotonous. The ballerina had no character whatsoever.

That night she saw him standing alone at the bar. He was drinking rum and seemed determined not to look her way. She stood next to him, ordered a drink. She touched his arm. Where are you going? he asked her. Nowhere, she said. What are you drinking? he asked. Beer, she said. He didn't look at her, he kept his eyes averted, he was not welcoming. The beer tasted bitter in her mouth. She had an urge to leave. It was dark in the bar, it seemed to her to be full of shadows that were more substantial than the people. The salsa band was playing but it sounded hollow to her ears. A woman in a tight dress walked by and his eyes travelled over her figure.

He was a passionate man, she knew this from before. She sipped her beer and remembered the first time he kissed her hard on the mouth. The moon had been full. Do you see the rabbit? he'd asked her. She'd laughed.

What are you saying? Then he'd explained that in this country there's a rabbit in the moon. No man, only a rabbit, he'd said. She found this a beautiful fact, but for the life of her she couldn't see the rabbit. That's because you see what you want to see, he told her. Who doesn't? she'd quipped. Those who see the rabbit, he said, and he tried again to point out the ears and whiskers and the skinny legs about to spring over the moon's edge into the dark and cloudy spaces of the universe. It had been an intense affair and once he told her it was too intense. Now his face was closed, shadows overcame his features. I'm leaving, she said.

At home she arranged flowers she picked up at the Tuesday Market. Gold lilies and small white star-shaped flowers that smelled like lilac, some lavender weed called, in translation, Turkey Spit and which referred to the substance in the corners of the eyes. It pleased her that there were words in Spanish for which there were only awkward English equivalents. Like the rabbit in the moon her gringa eyes refused to see. She wrote a postcard which began *Hola Amiga* wherein she discussed the rain and the color of the sky. She gazed at the ballerina and wondered if she should forget about it, throw it in the closet or give it away.

The day was balmy and beautiful. The orange bougainvillea on her patio twirled in the light breezes. She sat outside and sketched the rooftops, the blue dome and the orange tiles, the wrought iron railings and the laundry hanging from wires suspended between narrow walls. Someone had grown pink roses in a terra cotta planter and they persisted, full-blown, up a fat metal pipe. There were a few TV antennas and small piles of broken brick and stone and glass.

She ran into the palmist, Pamela, at the café. She was reading *Women's Wear* and a gray scarf tangled around her neck. How are you? she asked the palmist? I'm just fine, hon, said Pamela and she looked down at her magazine. She seemed unwilling to continue the conversation. She was studying a model who wore tights and a tuxedo jacket and boots and carried an enormous satchel. The caption read AT HOME OR ABROAD.

This encounter made her feel alienated and lonely. Despite the amazing beauty of the place, she felt as though she had no friends. She took the long way home and thought about her life, thought about changes she could possibly make.

She decided she would fix the ballerina painting after all. She would try to see what was there, not merely what she wanted to see. She envisioned it as she walked home—the new, fresh colors, the brush strokes. And if it resulted in a complete annihilation of the ballerina, so be it.

Once home, however, she lost her resolve. She drank a glass of red wine and watched the sun set over the lake. Everything is banal, she thought. She spilled red wine on her leg and watched it stain her skin. Everything is accidental, she thought. She hauled the ballerina painting from behind the sofa and dribbled red wine over what had been the background, where it ran off the painting, making no impression whatsoever.

That night she dreamed he came to her. He was carrying a vase of flowers. Stop painting! he commanded her. Then he sprouted wings and flew into a mirror. Symbolism! he shouted. She awoke in a sweat, feverish and with terrible stomach pains. You better take a stool sample in, advised her landlady.

It turned out to be typhoid. The stomach pains were more than she could bear and so she was hospitalized, drugged. Her nurse's name was Nancy. She wore a red wig. Don't worry, we are very expert at this disease, Nancy told her sourly. Lie still and I will keep the curtains closed. She received many injections at what seemed to be chaotic intervals and at one point she could have sworn he came to see her. He sat beside her bed and held her hand solemnly.

But all of this was mixed up with a dream she was having about a monkey who kept trying to skitter up a tree and couldn't. I'm so unhappy, she thought she told him. What if I die? When he laughed he showed his very bright teeth. I'm very thin, she remembered announcing to Nancy one morning. There are lots thinner than you, admonished Nancy. Her red wig had changed colors, it was now blonde. When she opened the curtains, the sunlight hit the eyes of the patient with such force it made her cough. They released her that morning. Don't drink, said Nancy. Don't go to parties.

She could hardly walk to the taxi and once inside she noticed that the leopard seat covers were stained with red wine. Not wine, said the driver. Blood. Does it disturb you? Because if so I'll give you a discount. Or some mota, your choice. Oh please, she said. Just take me home.

At home her landlady had baked her a loaf of seed bread. Welcome home, she said. This bread is for health. You're thin as a stick. A little crowd of well-wishers were waiting for her, including him and the beautiful artist from the class. Someone—a woman with a very heavy perfume—kissed her on the cheek. So glad you are still among us, she whispered. Pamela, the palmist.

Much later she realized that she had been foolish to fret over the ballerina painting. It would be discovered, after many years, in the back of a closet and she would look at it affectionately. Its nervous effort, its palimpsest of color and line and movement would seem, from this distance, to be perfectly expressive of that time, her sweet melancholy, her inconsolable self. Therefore, at that time, she would remember this time, and she would remember him, the man who had pointed out the rabbit in the moon. And it would seem to her now, so many years hence, that she had in fact actually seen the rabbit—its loopy ears, its misty half-smile, its rounded, fuzzy haunches about to leap off the face of the moon and soar down to earth—after all. But this perspective on the facts of her life would come much later.

THE BEETLE AND THE NUN

A WOMAN WITH LONG hair is walking through a five-hundred-year-old colonial building on her way to a literary reading. This building used to be a convent and so you must imagine both the woman in her up-to-date clothes and the nun who stood in the same spot centuries ago with her eyes downcast. The nun is watching the small course of a beetle wander on the old stones. She has thrown water on the stones and now the beetle must make its way among many small seas of water. It meanders, therefore, and this activity which is determined by happenstance rather than by the instinct of the beetle is fascinating to the nun who has worked all morning brushing the stones and rinsing them and before that pushing new seedlings into the dirt around the jacaranda. She watches without realizing she is watching; she watches without thinking. Where the beetle goes, around the green stone and circumventing the puddle at the end of the black stone, the nun goes too. In this sense the nun enters the consciousness of the beetle—she is everywhere with the beetle, in the moment of traveling, without her self-consciousness.

On the other hand, the woman with long hair who is wearing modern clothes—tights with red roses, a black knit shirt, silver earrings—is being watched by a man at a nearby table. This man is an artist and he watches her both with the eye of an artist and the eye of a prospective lover. He watches the shape of her ankles as she walks past and he watches the small movement at the corner of her mouth, an indication that she has seen him; and he watches her feet which step with purpose and with hesitation at the same time. Intuitively, the man knows (because he is an artist) that the woman is inclined to stop at his table, but that a force inside her compels her forward. It is this force in her that he falls in love with, right from the beginning: the force that moves her past him, again and again, against her will.

The nun who is watching the beetle loves, in the same way, when she has the leisure to reflect upon it, the beetle's independence from her own being despite her power over it. With one splash from the bucket she could annihilate the beetle, but the beetle takes its chances. If she could have the faith of the beetle her life would be perfect. But her faith is imperfect. When she prays she gets into tangles—whether she is resisting God or desiring Him too much she cannot from one moment to the other say. There seems to be no place in her mind which is free from the contamination of her will and yet it is exactly will which she admires in the beetle.

The man and the woman meet the same night at a cocktail party after the literary reading. He takes her breath away. There is something about the intensity in his face which draws her out of herself. Although she is usually shy with people she meets for the first time, she is direct with him and asks him to meet her somewhere. And he who is usually direct, especially with women, is shy with her. In fact, he is tempted to stand her

up. Hence, right away a power struggle ensues between them. This motif
will characterize their relationship, which turns out to be painful.

The nun sings a little song to herself before sleep and the others tell her
to hush. But this has been her habit from childhood and she is unable to
give it up. She is reluctant to renounce all that she must renounce—her
memories, especially the moods of childhood, the way a certain smell
or sound will take her there. On a deeper and more grievous level she is
reluctant to give up the person she used to be, the self who has taken her
to the convent and has pledged her life to God but who has also run in
the fields and filled her mouth with water and looped her body over the
body of a cow. Without that self she would feel not quite whole, but she
knows this is heresy because only God is capable of providing wholeness
to one of his daughters.

If the nun and the woman would meet they would recognize one another
as those who are passionate to excess.

When the man holds the woman in his arms he feels her overwhelming
desire, the mouth at the root of her desire, and this frightens him. Likewise, the other nuns avoid this Sister Claire, who is ardently sincere, to
the point of conceit. When the moon slides into the night sky the nun
and the woman will be standing at the same spot looking at the stars.
Because they feel that only here can they fathom their own insignificance, shrinking against the sky and the walls. In this way, they are able
to annihilate love.

Otherwise, although the woman loves the man, she is unable to surrender herself to him. Often, she forces her heart to harden in his presence.

For a while, when they first met, she became enthralled: she dreamt of him each night, she felt he was invading her dreams with his images; and when they made love she felt as though he had touched her soul. Afterwards she would run from him to her own home, her own bed and she would weep without knowing why. But now she barely thinks about him. She has come to the point that she can let him come and go and let herself come and go and they can wander past one another and in and out of one another's lives leaving barely a ripple on the surface. Now he is to her as a beetle is to a nun in a long ago century.

AT THE FIGHTS

I WENT TO THE bar and saw Jesus with his round face, his dimples and his big smile. In Leonardo's across the hall the fight was on: Chavez and a contender who butted him in the head and the fight was cancelled. A man told me if a boxer gets a head wound it's usually all over. They bleed too much. Chavez was pressing something to his head, or his trainer was. It seemed like he still wanted to fight but someone was arguing strenuously against continuing. Maybe his manager. They gave him the fight and the other guy looked tragic. He had a scar on his chin.

When I was born I had a birthmark on my chin, not really a disfiguration, but a little swelling where most people have an indentation. When it was operated on, I was left with a series of tiny lumps which formed a larger knotted scar. It wasn't a tragedy, I wasn't beautiful to begin with.

Jesus told me that inside he was dark. He had moody thoughts. He liked to live on the edge. He has an appealing gap between his front teeth which I commented on. Even so, I decided I didn't want to sleep with him.

The man in Leonardo's had slicked back hair and a ponytail. He motioned me over and put his arm around me. He explained boxing. It's a great sport, boxers are the gentlest guys in the world. They never get in bar fights. They're perfect gentlemen. The man smelled of sex. I could smell it on his breath. He leaned into me when he talked. Chavez looked disappointed. It must not be fulfilling to win a fight like that, by default. It doesn't matter, said the man. If you win, you win.

In the salsa bar Jesus had to pay for me. I left my money at home. I knew I didn't want to sleep with him but I let him pay. Como no. I pay for people sometimes. I gave Gabriel five pesos for a cab last week. It was raining and he didn't want to get wet. But I resented it. I didn't want to give him pesos for a cab. I walk, why can't he? But I gave him the pesos because he caught me off guard.

I tried to get into the spectacle of the fight. They were locked together, they were trading punches. I couldn't tell who was winning. It's actually pretty even, said the man, it's a good fight. Then Chavez got heat-butted. They showed it in slo-mo about five times. He swung at the other guy and the other guy ducked his head and then came up from under. Chavez's head was down. Then he swayed back, a little off balance, and put up his gloves. To show his remorse, the other guy, the contender, put his arms around Chavez. It was a touching scene. Still, I'm not much of one for boxing. I like a game where you can see the score.

Jesus begged me to dance with him. He made his eyes look pleading but I knew it was all an act. He said he'd been watching me a long time, he wanted to know me. Actually he wanted to fuck me and I knew this would not happen. He was dying to smoke a joint. He was dying to fuck me. He was dying to dance. He was a good dancer, it turned out. He had good rhythm and every once in a while he'd grab me by the hips and push me back and forth. Then I'd give a twirl. Only I hate to catch sight of myself in the salsa bar mirror. It's always a disappointment.

I said goodbye to the man in Leonardo's. Later, I saw him in the salsa bar. Hi, he said. Only I was sitting with Jesus. Jesus and I talked about the great drummer Jack DeJohnette and the great bass player Charlie Haden. Also Miles. Once Jesus met Miles at a party in New York. I was impressed. I'm not trying to impress you, he said. Oh no? I said. I was just teasing but he looked hurt. Just kidding, I said. But it didn't help. After that he was standoffish, aloof. But he kept touching me while he talked to other people. He touched my shoulders and my leg. Are you in love with Frank? he said. Who's Frank? I said. I honestly didn't know. He's the singer, he said. I guess he said this because I was watching the singer. No, I said, I'm not in love with Frank.

How about Gabriel? he said. Are you in love with him? Gabriel's a friend of mine, I said. I'm not in love with anyone. I wanted to go home. I pictured myself getting into bed and turning out the lights, putting on the relaxation tape the hypnotist gave me which begins, *Now that you've decided to listen to this tape.* She speaks very slowly like a record that's gone awry. She has long dark hair and wears eyeliner inside her lower lid. Our eyes are the same color, a muddy green.

I'm recovering from a divorce, I told Jesus. You always think people will understand. But they don't. They treat you as if you've gone nuts. They treat you as if you're bullshitting them. It's the truth, I said. He gave one of those shrugs. He was beginning to annoy me. I decided to leave even though he paid ten pesos to get me in. I'll walk you home, he said.

But then he decided not to walk me home. Good decision, I thought, since I knew I wouldn't sleep with him. Nevertheless, I was lonely when I got in the house. Only the cats were there. They crowded around me and rubbed up against my ankles. Glad to see me. Hi cats, I said. I was tired. I knew they'd keep me up, scratching in my hair and sitting on my chest. This goes on for hours sometimes and it was already past midnight. Some life, I thought. I poured a shot of tequila and downed it. Then I called a woman I hadn't spoken to in twenty-five years. Hello? she said. Guess who this is, I said. I can't imagine, she said. When I told her she gave a shriek.

I had to hold the phone away from my ear. I remember when you cut up your slip, she said. We'd been in high school together. I don't remember cutting up my slip, I said. Your voice sounds different, she said. You used to have a slight lisp. Yes, but I've corrected it, I said. I no longer talk with a lisp. Thank god, she said. That lisp got on my nerves, she said. It got on everyone's nerves, I said.

After my father had my chin operated on, he sent me to speech school. There I corrected my lisp. I had to learn to put the tongue on the roof of my mouth when pronouncing words like listen and stew, instead of off to the side and pushed up against my teeth. It wasn't that hard to correct the lisp. My father was pleased. Now you can become an actress, he said. He sent me to acting school where I learned to do improvisations. I learned to feign deep feeling. I can still do it. But I quit acting school because I didn't like the people. They were all weirdos. Their clothes were trashy. They did too much dope. I made one friend there called Hank and I married him. We had a child who died.

After the child died nothing was the same. The woods, which once looked beautiful to me now looked worn out and tired, as if they had been hanging around too long in the same place. He was a boy with red hair. He died falling out of a tree. For a year or two I was depressed, but then I came out of it. When I did nothing looked the same. Even my husband looked different—his hair, the shape of his body, the quality of his voice, the way he picked up a coffee cup, everything about him was unfamiliar. Now I'm divorcing him. He's having an affair with a twenty-one-year-old. She's not any better looking than I am but she's young. That counts for something, he said. It sure does, I said. We toasted on it. Coronas. The divorce agreement is very fair. We each get everything we came into the marriage with. Otherwise we split it down the middle. I get half a house. Which half? I said.

I talked to my friend on the phone for 20 minutes. At two bucks an hour that's forty bucks. I can't say it was worth it. I hadn't talked to her in 25 years but she didn't have much to say. I said, What's new? And she said, Nothing. Then she told me about this video she watched recently starring Meryl Street and Roseanne Barr. She told me every detail, frame by frame. She even remembered some of the dialogue. Finally I said I had to hang up.

Then I thought I'd wrap up the night, have another shot of tequila, carry the cats up to bed. They weren't my cats but I said I'd take care of them in exchange for living in the house. Part of that included sleeping with them. While I was at it, I ate a few tortillas and a mango. In the next courtyard a big party was going on. They were paying Nueva Trouva music very loud. The men were singing along and their voices were off-key. I didn't hear any women's voices. They must have been pretty drunk. On the wall of the courtyard a stray cat was making the ugly noises a cat in heat makes. I was tired but there was too much noise for sleep. To top it all off dogs were barking and someone was setting off firecrackers.

I rummaged in the cupboard for more food, maybe some crackers or a can of beans. But there wasn't anything but salt and red wine vinegar. Around this time, I began to regret leaving the salsa bar. Watching the fight had been interesting. I didn't think I liked boxing, but Chavez and the contender had nobility, as the man in Leonardo's said. They weren't intelligent but they knew something about life. They knew that life was made up of wins and losses, and occasional dirty dealings. The whole thing reduced to essentials.

After I dropped out of acting class Hank and I moved to the suburbs. We bought an old bar and decorated it with crates and cushions. Then I got pregnant. When Hank went to work I'd take long walks in the woods. I didn't know the names of anything—trees, wildflowers, mosses that grew on the banks of the gorge—all was a mystery to me. I never thought about it much, but I guess I was happy. When you think about it you're not happy as a rule. I used to throw sticks in a stream. If the stick disappeared it meant my luck would run out; if it floated along in the current it meant

I'd be saved. I had an idea of salvation from the Jehovah's Witnesses who used to knock on the door every Saturday morning. Two black women, Edna and Edna May. It was funny that they had the same name. We used to give them fifty cents for *The Watchtower*. Then we'd talk about plants.

Now I'm taking care of plants for the people who own this house. I keep forgetting to water them. Even when I remember, it's hard to make myself. When the child died I threw out our plants. One of them was a begonia that Edna May had rooted in a glass of water. A fire begonia, she called it. It grew into a large plant with variegated leaves and red blooms the size of soup spoons. My son had red hair. He sat in a snuggly on my back when I walked in the woods. When he got older he slept in one of the crates for a week. He said he liked it there, it was better than his bed.

Jesus told me he was married for nine years. This was earlier in the evening. We were exchanging information, trying to get to know each other. Nine years, he said, it was tough. Why? I said. Sometimes I feel I'm taking a survey. I was a musician, on the road, there were so many women around, you know how it is. Did you have a lot of affairs? I asked him. Not really, he said. How about her? I asked. Was she lonely? Did she complain that you were never home? Who knows, he said. We never talked that much.

Next we discussed sarcasm. I am very sarcastic, he said. My brain works fast. I am very quick witted and sarcastic. I said you probably shouldn't tell people that. Why? he said. It's better to let people draw their own conclusions. Are you being sarcastic? he said. As a rule, I'm not sarcastic, I said. Then what are you? he asked. I said I didn't know. The secret of life, he said, is knowing exactly who you are and what you want. Right now, I want you. He stroked my knee.

I didn't think I knew what I wanted until I saw Chavez and the contender slugging away at each other. Afterwards, they hugged. That's it, I thought, and I looked around the room for someone to sweep me away.

NUMBER FOUR

A LEXANDER IS DATING THREE women in town. He tells her this. They happen to be dancing in the salsa bar. *One two stop, one two stop, shift the weight, it's all in the knees.* Oh, she says. Does that make me number four? He says, I just like to be open and honest. I value sincerity. Yes, you may very well be number four.

Who wouldn't be flattered? she says. She's shy and resorts to sarcasm as a defense mechanism. He holds her firmly around the waist, dips and turns. The hip movement doesn't come naturally to her. She's not sure if she likes him. His shirts are wrong. He has a weak jaw. He sweats.

I have to accept myself for what I am, he says. What are you? she asks. She is seriously interested because it has not been in the realm of her experience to meet men who can answer this question. Most of them are vague or mistaken. Her last boyfriend saw himself as sensitive and caring. Moreover, he overused those words when describing himself. But aside from his way of fawning over small children, she found him unredeemingly mean. He refused to let her wear his funky thrift-store shirts and boycotted movies she recommended. When she cried he left home. When she became depressed he left town.

Now she is dancing with a man who dates three women. Something asks: Will this make you happy?

The good thing about the man—Alexander—is that he is the right age. He is approximately her age. He has an ex-wife, grown kids. He's suffered: she can sense this in his posture and in the way he talks to her, cautious, wounded-like. Plus, he has jowls and crow's feet. Therefore, he is not likely to balk at a caesarean scar or a sagging boob.

I'm a sincere enough guy, he says, but I can't seem to sustain a relationship for more than two years. That's not very long, she says. What does that say about your capacity for love? I've been madly in love, blissfully happy for, say, six months. Then I lose interest, he says. He propels her into a half turn, catches her eye and smiles charmingly. He has a good mouth. Time's running out, she says.

His business is imports. Imports? she says. What kind of imports? He refuses specificity. Drug dealer, she thinks.

This is their first date. In his car, which is creepily devoid of human debris, he leans over the plush armrest and kisses her. Gentle. Maybe he touches her hair. She wonders how it would be to be number four, whether it would solve any of her problems. Danger, she decides.

———

She is renting a house high above the city. There are exactly one hundred stone steps of varying heights and stabilities that must be climbed, often in total darkness, in order to reach it. But it has a 360-degree view of the city, as advertised, and three terraces from which to watch sunsets. Only she never goes to the terraces at sunset. Usually she is reading or eating. Occasionally she attends to bodily hygiene. But it's hard. The hot water heater is continually going out and the light bulb above the only mirror is ineffective. She quit wearing makeup and discovered that her hair, though unclean, is actually more manageable.

She's a photographer who's down here on assignment, but she's finding it hard to work. Her editor Frances has said, Do what you want, your own vision type-of-thing is what we're after. There's too much freedom in this assignment, she'd complained. Why don't you give me a few parameters? Just go, said Frances, have fun, take pictures. What a deal, said everyone when she told them. But she was stuck. Everything photographable had already been photographed: the washerwomen laboring over the tiled tubs, the beggar children in their little plastic shoes, the cathedrals, the old men in sombreros. All clichés. Briefly she'd thought about photographing the tourists themselves, their pot bellies and cameras, their shopping sprees, bad manners, and pathos—but the idea of tracking tourists makes her head ache. Also she is tired of irony.

She is preparing enchiladas when he calls. Yo, he says. Did you call me? How could I call you, I don't have your number, she says. Well you better write it down, he says. He gives it to her and hangs up.

She goes to the terrace to witness the sunset. It just rained. The sun is sinking below a blue cloud. The sky is streaked with pink and orange. Everything else is green and turquoise. She can't seem to get a handle on any of it.

It's true, she's happier here but she had been miserable there. Therefore, she is less miserable at this point in time, though not necessarily happy. She tells this to Diego the cat, a creature she feeds intermittently and hates consistently. He had been unwholesome when they met, with a swollen, festering eye and chunks of fur torn from his back, as if by a bear. He was draped lethargically over her stone wall, giving her the evil eye. I find you loathsome, she said. But she gave him cereal anyway and in minutes he recovered. Now she asks him: Why don't you go to Chiapas and join the revolution?

———

She is making mole when Alexander drops by. The armpits of his orange silk shirt have little half-moons of sweat underneath and he is panting, out of breath. Fuck, he says. That's some climb. He brings a bottle of Chilean cabernet. Nice, she says, taking the wine. I'm making mole.

He helps her chop a few things and he feeds the cat; he admires the plants which come with the house. Not a good sign. Her most recent husband was good with plants and made them flourish obscenely. After a while, houseplants crowded every inch of their living room. They crept over the furniture, diminished the artwork, and there were always microscopic bugs hovering. She is into spare design, minimalism. She likes a fine wooden table in a bare room. Her idea of hell is unruly greenery tickling the back of her neck while watching TV.

Tell me about these women, she says over mole. What women? he says. Number one, two, and three, she says. My competition. Ah, he says. I don't exactly have them ranked. What do you take me for? Anyway, I worry about them, their futures. This is a man's town, so they have no one but me. He blots the corners of his lips with a paper towel. Good mole, he says. Did you make it from scratch? Of course, she says. What do you take me for?

Ah ha ha, he says. I should have known you'd be into cooking. Your type.

What types are the others?

They're attentive, nurturing, very kind women.

Are they all blondes? she asks, a sudden intuition.

Yes, he says, embarrassed.

On the radio a salsa band, as luck would have it. How about it? says Alexander. Together they step and shuffle and bump into a table. They try again and knock over a plant. Still, they keep going, one two, bend the knees, and even though it's supposed to be automatic, her hips won't do that thing. I'm too old to start, she thinks. It's too hard, she tells him.

Afterwards he caresses her neck. You're sweet, he says. I'm getting to like you. Hmm, she says. Recently, she's had an ex-husband and an ex-boyfriend, and distantly, more exes, too numerous to specify. Right now, everyone looks like an ex to her. She sees them in the past; or rather she experiences her time with them as though it is already in her past, as though she is remembering the start of another rotten relationship. Those words—*I'm getting to like you*—therefore give her a chill. It's unfortunate that this happens to her lately. Bad for her social life.

I'm tired, she says. Making the mole was exhausting. I like you too, she adds as an afterthought. Unconvincing. He is finishing his wine, checking his watch. She longs for his hands on her shoulders and in her hair. But it's too late.

———

In El Jardin she searches for an image. What is it she wants? That which is capable of disclosing suffering. The heart of suffering instead of the surface accoutrements which always appear false: the beggar children's dirty faces. One approaches and here is how she looks: black hair which hangs crookedly against her neck in a thick jagged line. Brown eyes in which a crafty abjectness has been planted. Dame un peso por favor.

Once she heard someone say, *You could give every peso you have and still it would not make a dent.* The eye of the beholder—what did it mean? And her eye, for what did it search? Her husband had once said: You'll never find what you're searching for. Whatever you want, it's not here in this human world. At the time she thought he was being mean-spirited, but now, in retrospect, it has the chilling resonance of truth.

The child implores and she gives. Any attempt to communicate one's suffering results in these travesties. The child races off. The clatter of her shoes on the stones is like the flap of birds overhead who descend, competitive, for one piece of bread. She points her camera but she can't shoot. This is a third-world country, she thinks.

It is a manner of style, of finding the right tone. Sometimes it's the matter of prayer: to implore or to seek or to see: all are simpatico verbs.

And because of who she is, because something has been communicated, other children gather around her. Like the birds they descend, four or five or seven of them, with plugs of snot in their noses. The littlest taps her knee. Por favor, he says. She could give away all her pesos and it would not make a dent.

Instead she fishes for a fountain pen from her bag. The ink in the pen is black and she gives each child a little dot on the palm of their hand. Then, on the littlest, an X. Thrilled, the children demand more dots, more X's. Here in this city more is never enough.

Sometimes she thinks the problem is in the eye of the beholder: herself. When she was married she and her husband gave annually to AIDS in return for which they attended a Halloween party. This was before the cure. It was great fun; men in drag swishing through the jack o'lanterns, her best friend Mike always wore sapphire blue high heels and a mink stole. The people with AIDS never attended the ball; they were at home vomiting and turning into skeletons. But at the Halloween ball, this was not on your mind.

She is thinking, I screw up every relationship before it begins. I cannot locate even my own sorrow. Also, there's the salsa problem, which has become a metaphor for her state of mind.

Then a bird shits on her head. I hate these fucking birds, she tells the kids. They are laughing, doubled over, as she wipes the drooly mess with a Kleenex. Scat, she says, but they continue to laugh, holding onto each other with their dirty hands, besides themselves with laughter, dirty hands on dirty arms and sleeves and knees. She opens her wallet and dumps all the pesos on the sidewalk. It will not make a dent.

———

At home Diego is ill. He has resumed his former lethargy, only worse, crouched in a glass-filled corner of the terrace with his eyes half closed, scraggly tail sweeping the wall in a slow circle. When he sees her, he whimpers but doesn't move. She offers him leftover pasta and pieces of ham. He turns his head, refusing, then lets it sink to his paws. He screams loudly, a sound that fills her with horror. She asks him: Are you really sick or is this an act?

She calls the vet, a Dr. Roboso, who asks, What are his symptoms?

He is listless, he won't eat anything, he's screaming.

What do you mean, screaming? Cats, as a general principle, don't scream.

Take my word for it, Dr. Roboso, this cat is screaming.

How old is this cat?

I have no idea. It's a stray.

A stray cat? If everyone were to call about stray cats I'd be a rich man, says Dr. Roboso with some disapproval. Anyway you need to get a urine sample. Get a syringe, look for urine.

That's impossible. I can't do it.

What do you mean you can't do it?

I mean it boggles my mind just thinking about it.

I'll be there at five.

———

Dr. Roboso arrives precisely at five p.m. carrying a beige plastic cat cage and a vinyl briefcase. He's wearing running shoes and shorts and appears to be about 19. After a brief handshake—his hand is small, tender—he goes straight to Diego who continues to slump in a corner of the terrace, moaning loudly.

He may have eaten a rat, he says. Cats do that, then they get block-ages. He probes Diego's stomach gently and Diego's moans increase in volume. Yes, there's a blockage, says Dr. Roboso. Would you like to pay for an operation?

No, she says. Then: How much?

Roboso shrugs: It's expensive. Surgery, anesthetic, after care. I wouldn't bother if I were you. He is nobody's cat, not even yours. When you leave, he'll die anyway of neglect. That's life. Roboso was washing his hands in the kitchen sink.

Maybe you're right, she says. And something inside her knuckles under, hopeless. When Roboso leaves she opens a bottle of wine and shuts the patio door against the cat's noisy suffering and against the equally irritating sunset.

——

That night she sees Alexander out with another woman. She's a lanky blonde and they sit on bar stools, side by side, staring companionably into space. Then they get up to salsa. The woman is an expert; her hips move softly to the beat, her knees incline and snap, her footwork is precise without being forced. She is wearing a gray dress which seems to float on her body and Alexander's hand on her waist looks as if it belongs. He winks at her across the room and gestures for her to join them. She's not inclined to do this.

For one thing, she's alone, and it's embarrassing to be single when the only man who asks you out is with another woman. He should realize this. For another, she's trying to read. The light is poor, but the waiters have been obliging, seating her at a table under one of the big fan-lights near the kitchen. She is reading a book about Mexican history and culture and the author is asserting the complexity of the national character: *Today, in strictly ethnic terms, 90 percent of Mexicans are mestizos, but as individuals they remain trapped by the contradictions of their own parentage. They are both the sons of Cortés and Cuauhtémoc, yet they are neither Spanish or Indian.*

How strange to have at the root of one's being both the consciousness of the conqueror and the consciousness of the victim, she is thinking, and even as she thinks this, she absently accepts the solicitations of the waiter, refilling her coffee cup, emptying her ashtray, short and indigenous like most of his class. And this makes her think of Diego who, when she left for the night, had stopped moaning and had given her a dim, pain-filled look as she set a bowl of water beside him.

She is thinking these thoughts when Alexander catches her eye and motions insistently. She smiles weakly and leaves her seat, but she is not happy about it.

Hey, she says, I was reading. We can see that, says Alexander, amused. The woman whose name is Tina seems amused as well.

Good book? says Alexander. His eyes are very blue, she just notices this fact for the first time. They quite catch her by surprise.

History, she says, but since there's a lull in the talk, she feels compelled to tell him about Diego.

Oh, says Tina. Her eyes fill and Alexander pats her kindly on the shoulder. Tina loves animals, he explains.

I do, says Tina, sniffing. I'm a sap for sad animal stories. Maybe you should put him to sleep.

This, in fact, had never occurred to her.

At midnight she arrives at the vet's home, breathless, Diego swaddled in a striped blanket, almost unconscious. Dr. Roboso comes to the door drinking a Pepsi, still in his jogging outfit. He looks at her sternly.

It's very late, he says.

I'm sorry, Dr. Roboso.

Do you want the operation? he asks.

And in that moment she decides something she hadn't thought she would decide and the decision, once she makes it, seems exactly right. Don't worry, it's a simple procedure, says Roboso, lifting the swaddled cat from her arms. I'll call you tomorrow.

———

The next time she sees Alexander she's sitting on the pink wall surrounding the park searching for an image. It's late afternoon and the sun is fading rapidly. She's been there for hours, camera poised, looking. There are the wide, flat leaves like jungle leaves and the crop of pink lilies with their pale complicated centers. There are the birds flying noisily from branch to flower to the broken hand of a statue. There are two women dragging their bundles in black plastic bags and their children who follow eating melted orange popsicles. There is a stone fountain with no water. There are the washerwomen's clothes drying nearby on the same stone wall, tee shirts and jeans and aprons with faded designs. There are boys playing basketball on the far court without their shirts on and a couple of lovers secluded under a tree, kissing.

Then there is Alexander walking up the cobbled hill in the half-light with a chocolate cake, and this is the image that appeals to her the most. Hold it, she says, as he makes his way toward her, and she raises the camera and shoots ten in a row, fast and pro-ish. She gets his look of amazement and then his grin and she gets the chocolate cake tilting dangerously to one side and his relief as he rights it, and she gets one where he looks tired, a little sad, sweaty, exhausted as she is, by life itself. By all the effort it takes.

You're a nut, he says when he reaches her. Was that for real?

Of course it was real, Alexander. It's the best thing I've shot all week.

Huh, he says. His eyes drift toward the trees and then back to her. I guess I must look pretty stupid. He lifts the cake and shrugs.

Not at all, it was wonderful, she says. She wants to reassure him, to tell him something nice. She smiles. Whose birthday?

Tina's. He grins sheepishly.

Tina? One of the many women of Alexander.

That part got complicated, stressful, he says.

Tell me, she says. He rests the cake on the pink wall and wipes his forehead with a yellow kerchief. They started talking about me, all three women, comparing notes. It's such a small town. There were feelings, you know how it is, hurt feelings. And so I had to choose. He pauses and gives a kid with a runny nose a peso. You were right it couldn't last long.

And you chose Tina.

Right, he says. I chose Tina. He flexes his eyebrows. One is better than two, you were right.

That's great, Alexander, she says, and she means it.

I should be off, he says, checking his watch. Tina. She's making pasta. What happened with the cat, by the way?

The cat's fine, she tells him. He had an operation and now he's better.

Geez, says Alexander. You must really like that cat.

Yeah, she says. It's my cat.

She watches him trudge up the hill, the cake on the flat of his right hand, his pale silk shirt spotted with damp across the back. She watches the sun sink below the horizon, the sky growing wild and then tame, filling with darkness. The moon is a bright sliver, and the dazzle of fireworks in celebration of St. Carmen, spray across the night like shooting stars. She is watching all of this, thinking of Alexander and Tina feeding each other cake, of Diego sleeping peacefully on her pillow, of Chiapas and revolutionary fervor, and of the children's beautiful faces laughing and laughing. And then she is thinking about salsa—how hard it is to learn a new dance, to get the feet to work with the body until it becomes unconscious and graceful, like life. Oh when will it happen?

EVE'S HAIR, A CORRIDA

1

Eve has very long hair. When she's writing about the revolution in her notebook, her hair falls over her eyes like a veil and makes the oppression of the proletariat seem vague, as if it had not really occurred. The same thing happens in conversation, in which case the other conversant sees only the tip of Eve's nose and a corner of her right eye and her teeth flashing in between her words like punctuation.

Eve is not a beautiful woman, she has only her hair, which is dark brown with little ripples of gray running through it, behind which very small ears are secluded. According to Eve's mother her ears are her best feature and it distresses her that her dear daughter insists on covering them with all that hair. Not that there aren't times when Eve wears her hair in a bun or a ponytail. But those times are few and far between and usually before the night is out she becomes self-conscious and unfastens the clip or barrette or rubber band, or pulls out the hair pins, and allows her hair to fall in its usual manner, which is slanted across her face like a shadow.

Eve is not unwise about the implications of her attachment to her hair. She knows, for example, that hair is a metonymy for sexuality and she knows that hiding behind her hair the way she does, using her hair with its knots and tangles and voluminousness as a screen, might also suggest her sexual ambivalence, her shame, her fear of intimacy. When she tries to imagine herself without long hair she experiences nausea and anxiety which alerts her to the fact that hair, for her, is not unmixed with childhood traumas, being forced to march in processions, always behind the boys, carrying little baskets of rose petals and being photographed by gringo tourists who have no idea who she really is.

Eve is a revolutionary who has never seen a revolution. Each day of her life she prays for the revolution to occur, for an army of passionate guerillas to overrun the city with red bandannas, machetes, and automatic weapons. These days, which are the turbulent days before the election, Eve is more hopeful than ever.

> Declaration by Zapatista Army of National Liberation: *Democratic change is the only alternative to war. Whether by suicide or by firing squad, the death of the current political system is a necessary condition for a transition to democracy in our nation.*

Presently, Eve is out of work. For quite some time she managed the front desk at an upscale hotel. This was not a difficult job, involving only the simplest calculations and the most rudimentary courtesies to guests. The hotel was always swarming with conventioneers with plastic name tags and expectant faces that quickly changed into dull disappointment as the convention progressed. At this phase, the phase of disappointment when the sought-after adventure, the fantasized liaison with an exotic beauty with the face of an angel and the body of a Playboy model, had not transpired, the hotel's cocktail hour would double its take and there would be many drunken and more or less pathetic men wandering around. Many's the time Eve would be approached at her station and invited to a hotel room by an unsteady plastic surgeon or computer software salesman. Luckily, she knew how to fend off these advances with tact and courtesy, even though she wished she had the guts to slit their throats.

Then, rather unexpectedly, she was fired. It had, supposedly, to do with her hair, which she refused to tie back in what Mr. Perla the manager called a professional manner. We cannot, said Mr. Perla righteously, have hairs on the accounting ledgers, hairs in the coffee cups, hairs on the leaves of the fern. Everywhere I look there are hairs! cried Mr. Perla, throwing up his soft hands. Therefore, you are fired! On a deeper level it had to do with Eve rebuffing the advances of Mr. Perla, a man in his 50s, with a pot belly, a wife, and an odd smell, like ham.

Eve's mother, Miracula, was very upset when she lost her job. Miracula is a tiny woman, with feet the size of postcards and a head that can squeeze easily between the wrought iron grillwork on the living room window. To counterbalance her insignificance in space, she has developed a calculating nature which enables her to persecute others. For example, she has the capacity to maintain a stony silence for weeks. At these times, there is a corresponding acceleration of domestic industry, the ripping apart of cupboards, the shaking of rugs into the bougainvillea, the scouring of pots and pans that haven't been used in twenty years. Since it drives Eve crazy and makes her feel guilty at the same time, this behavior is very effective. It's true that Eve's income is important to the family, but doesn't Miracula understand that when the revolution comes, which it will after August 21, the entire family will be liberated? You would think she'd have a little faith in the future, but no, she would rather torment Eve.

Picture Miracula moving resentfully through the house, like an enraged cat, tearing up worn stockings and shuffling noisily through newspapers, and there is Eve with her hair in her eye, jotting a note here and there about the life of Che Guevara, her hero, finding inspirational slogans for the coming months, growing more and more irritated at her mother's behavior and simultaneously feeling worse and worse about herself, her value as a member of society.

> Octavio Paz: *We do not know where evil begins, if in words or in things, but when words are corrupted and meanings become uncertain, the sense of our acts and words is also uncertain. The history of man can be reduced to a history of the relation between words and thought.*

Ideas like these make their ways with increasing frequency into the consciousness of Eve, as she studies revolutionary thought. Clearly, there is a way to be victorious in any situation, but it takes careful planning and patience. Action, not words! Once in power, of course, one can be a fool. One might cover oneself with gold and execute one's citizens.

Revolution, on the other hand ... here Eve pauses and writes down the names of famous guerillas: *Albino García Ramos, Francisco Javier Mina, Nicolás Romero, Pedro José Méndez, Francisco "Pancho" Villa, Emiliano Zapata.*

Eve's boyfriend is a tough-faced man called Frank and he sells cars—Toyotas, Mercurys, American and Japanese alike. He and Eve have been together four years and it has become one of those relationships that persists out of habit rather than passion. She has always suspected him of sleeping with tourists, but this no longer gives her pain. Let him screw tourists all he wants! Eve is about to be liberated by history.

Briefly, these are the facts of Eve's life. I haven't given a fuller rendition of the character of Frank because he is receding, even as I write this, from Eve's line of vision. If they were in the famous painting of Velásquez,

Eve would be foreground and center in the place of the Princess Maria Christina and Frank would be a fold in the drapery.

2

Miracula is bending over the small metal wastepaper basket next to Eve's ankles. She has plunged in her hand and is rustling the papers inside and banging the sides of the metal as she does so. Eve is trying to blot out these sounds with difficulty. She is trying to imagine a conclave of revolutionaries in their mountain camp, crouched over a large, crudely drawn map of the country. They are smoking cigarettes, perhaps some mota; occasionally their laughter erupts, like gunfire, because the atmosphere is tense, filled with the possibility of victory:

Ignacio Ramírez:
Life is not life, but prison, in which want
and pain and lamentation pine in vain;
pleasure flown, who is afraid of death?

Isn't it ironic that the lethal becomes picturesque as time passes? What allows us to do this is language itself, which means that language allows us to hide the truth.

So many discoveries Eve is making!

In a few minutes her mother will slam a plate of spaghetti on the table and clear her throat loudly which is the signal for Eve to come to dinner.

Tonight, Eve's mother is wearing a bathrobe which she calls a housecoat and Eve is also wearing a bathrobe which she calls a kimono. They eat in silence. Miracula smacks her food loudly, however, and has taken to clanging the cutlery. Well, Eve says finally, haven't we had enough of this? I'm not the one who lost a high-paying job due to negligence, says Miracula, amazingly breaking her two-week silence. That hair has been the death of us both. Look, you have a piece of pasta in it right now. I'm not cutting my hair, Miracula, says Eve, I don't care what you say. They go on like this for quite some time, but at least they are talking.

Frank is wearing a dark blue polyester suit with a pink shirt, a striped tie, an alligator belt, brown shoes with little buckles, socks with dots on them. Frank! cries Miracula, who adores him. I see she's talking again, says Frank, throwing a newspaper on the table, his jacket across a chair. She wants me to cut my hair, says Eve. She doesn't care what Frank thinks, what Miracula thinks, or who thinks what. She wishes she could blot them out of her life like some people, great revolutionary leaders like Lenin or Stalin for example, blot out entire villages. Don't cut your hair, Baby, says Frank. Your hair is your greatest asset. That's what I think, says Eve. Any spaghetti left? says Frank. He has a look on his face that repulses Eve—the look of a greedy dog.

It occurs to Eve that there's not a person in the entire world that she actually likes. This thought makes her wonder if she's suicidal. Or homicidal.

Eve has her nightlight on. Frank is snoring alongside of her. A lock of his dark hair is twisted on the pillow and Eve has the urge to snip it off.

3

One month after Eve is fired, Mr. Perla comes to call. He is wearing the same odor he always wears: ham. When he enters the house to Eve's stiffly holding the door ajar, Miracula yells from another room, What's cooking? This is the effect of Mr. Perla's smell. Perhaps he is used to it.

Mr. Perla, it turns out, wants to hire Eve back. He is sorry, he really is, that he had to let her go in the first place, but sometimes you can't predict the things that are going to turn out to be mistakes. Mr. Perla is sitting on the edge of the green sofa. His knees are pointing out and he gesticulates nervously with his little hands as he speaks. He licks his lips.

In short, Eve, he says with a certain amount of formality, I would like to rehire you with a small raise as compensation for your trouble. And, he adds with an ingratiating smile at Miracula, for any trouble or pain this may have caused your dear mother.

Eve is happy to be back at the hotel. Her whole life runs more smoothly when she has a job, no matter what the job is, she realizes. For the first week or two she smiles generously at the tourists, and she is cordial and even merry with her co-workers. She doesn't bring her pamphlets to work, the way she used to, and she is altogether more cheerful-seeming and well adjusted. Everybody likes her. Mr. Perla shows his pleasure by inviting her for profiteroles in his private office. Mira Eve, he says, standing too close to her, you scratch my back, I'll scratch yours. He takes her hair in his soft hands and sweeps it above her head. I like your neck, he says. Let us see your neck more often, Eve, he says. Oye Perla, she says, knocking his hands away, you smell disgusting, like ham. Also, your days are numbered. Then she scoops up the last profiterole and leaves the room, banging the door behind her.

Amazingly, Perla does not fire her.

4

Manuel N. Flores:
And Suddenly
a quivering kiss was heard, and Paradise
trembled with love . . .

In short, everything goes well for Eve until she meets Tingo, the man who handles international reservations and who has begun to flirt outrageously with her. He is shorter than she is but very sexy with heavy lidded, conspiratorial eyes that never seem to move. Best of all, he is a revolutionary. When she walks down the hall it is his habit to pull her roughly into a room and take her mane of hair in one hand and tug it back from her forehead. Then, as he leans in to kiss her on the lips, he whispers the names of famous revolutionaries. *For Zapata*, he says and he sticks his tongue into her mouth. *Viva Marcos*, he says as he pinches her nipple through her shirt. This kind of behavior takes her breath away.

At home she is calmer and more tolerant with Miracula who is herself in a rare mood of contentment. Only Frank seems out of sorts, sensing perhaps that Eve's high spirits have nothing to do with him. He is home earlier these days and occasionally proffers gifts to Eve and her mother. These include a toaster oven, a key chain with a photo of Jennifer Lopez, and a two-liter jug of French cologne. Eve is unmoved by any of these gifts, pecking Frank perfunctorily on the cheek and tossing whatever it is aside with contempt.

She has taken to spending a lot of time in front of the mirror, re-arranging her hair—in topknots, French twists, braids on either side like a fräulein—trying on different eyeliners and rouges. I'm busy right now Frank, please don't disturb me for a while. She says this with an uncustomary haughtiness and Frank waits sullenly in the bedroom, pacing from bureau to bed and window where he gazes out at the little stand with the red awning that sells the best burritos in the city. Ok! he yells finally, rapping sharply at the bathroom door, I'll be on my way then. And Eve opens the door a crack and says Luego with barely a smile and a distracted look on her face.

She has fallen in love with Tingo. Everything about him has become precious to her: his torpid eyes, his hair which he wears wetted back like the telenovela star that played Pancho Villa in the miniseries, his white shirts that smell like flowers. Like Eve, he is these days in a revolutionary fervor. At night he meets with his compadres in a place so secret he is under pain of death to disclose it. He tells her that when the new republic comes, she'd better be ready for them. Freedom, he says, is circling the house like a fox. Like a fox? says Eve. Why a fox? It will be better for you if you don't ask stupid questions, he tells her sharply. But then he runs his fingers through her hair and says, This, this hair is freedom. He buries his face in it and inhales fiercely with his nose.

How could love be connected to revolution, she writes in her notebook, *unless it be its opposite?* Because love is making Eve feel weak-willed and soft. When she fantasizes about the revolution she can only think of what blouse will match the camouflage jacket and of making out with Tingo under a jungle thicket. When the revolution comes, she hopes and she prays that Tingo will not go off with a group of strangers into Chiapas or something. If he ever leaves the city, she thinks she will kill herself.

Eve dreams Tingo comes to her room and sits on the side of the bed and smooths her hair, saying Okay, it's okay, I'm with you now my darling, forever. I will not leave, fuck the revolution, we have each other.

5

Sor Juana:
This torment of love
that is in my heart,
I know I feel it
and know not why.

Tingo has become inconsistent with his attentions. One day he will make it his business to stroll by the reception desk every half hour or so, stopping to let his eyes wander towards the V in her shirt, and to whisper in a low intense voice: You are the only one who understands history. These others are fools. Then on the next day he'll hardly speak to her and when she clears her throat or drums her fingernails to get his attention, he'll turn to her with a look of mild surprise and annoyance on his face.

What do you want? he'll say. I'm a little busy now, Eve, he'll say. Then she feels this way: as if she's been punched in the stomach with a steel fist, as if her head will burst with her tears, as if she will run raging from the room and hurl herself under a truck.

Eve is more in love than ever.

With Miracula and Frank she behaves like a bitch, going to her room without eating or talking to anyone except to say Shut up or Leave me alone. She has begun to hate everything about herself—especially her hair. I hate my hair, she'll say to Frank at night. I think I'll cut it off. If only I could think of a style, I'd cut it right away. Don't ever cut your hair, Baby, Frank says. He's stroking her arm in a kind way, trying to kiss her neck, but his touch these days repulses her. The way his legs are crossed on her bed repulses her. The line of dirt under his fingernails repulses her. Why are you here every night, Frank? It's not as if we're married.

Eve is behaving so badly that Miracula decides it's time for one of her snits. Usually two weeks is enough to bring Eve around. But she barely gets through the first maddening night when her sister Lily comes to the house in distress. Lily is the glamourous aunt of Eve; she wears beautiful silk clothes and is very thin, as thin as a model, and she has long red plastic fingernails. Tonight, Lily's makeup is smeary because she is in the middle of a tragedy. Miracula, read my palm, please. I need to know the events of two weeks hence and possibly one month or two after that. She thrusts her palm into Miracula's face. I'm eating dinner, if you have your eyes still left in your head, Lily, after all those tears, says Miracula. Have some beans and an egg. I can't eat, says Lily, I can't sleep. Love, says Miracula. It's hell, says Lily. She is wearing all black tonight, a black blouse with little black triangles on it, a black chiffon skirt, black gloves, and a black mantilla. I hate myself is all I can say, Miracula. It is up to you to save me. Eve watches this scene with great interest. The phrase *love is hell* sticks in her mind.

Love is hell, she writes in her notebook.

Manuel Gutiérrez Nájera:
A fathomless abyss is human pain.
Whose eye has ever pierced to its black depths?

Love is revolution, she writes. *So many of the same qualities are shared by love and revolution that one wonders why they bother to make two words for these situations.* She adds the words of Octavio Paz: *The world of heroes and gods is no different from the world of men: it is a cosmos, a living whole in which the movement is called justice, order, destiny.* Her notebook is a map of human longings and failures, including her own. Depressing. Action is required!

6

Monday: Eve is wearing a white tank with a necklace made of amethysts and pearls, a necklace which dips charmingly into the curve of the tank, barely grazing the tops of her breasts which are cradled in a push-up bra. She is also wearing a long red skirt, suede sandals, and a gold anklet. When Tingo strolls by the reception desk, he makes a motion for her to follow, and she ignores him.

Tuesday: Eve is wearing a Japanese kimono printed with hyacinths, black espadrilles, a bracelet made of mahogany, and a camellia behind one ear. She is out by the pool talking to the maintenance team, a group of lifeguards with overdeveloped muscles. In the corner of her eye she spots Tingo needlessly arranging the white plastic lounge furniture. She gives him a brief but dazzling smile and continues her discussion, making sure to bat her eyes, toss her hair, and extend her leg from the kimono and prop it on a glass-topped table so that it may be admired to the thigh.

Wednesday: Eve is wearing hip-huggers, a silk shirt unbuttoned to the cleavage, boots and fat silver earrings. When Tingo pulls her into a room for a kiss she tosses her head away from him and emits, to her astonishment, a throaty chuckle. You are causing me so much trouble, he says petulantly. What? says Eve, immediately self-conscious. Ysssh, he says, biting her neck. Ouch, she says.

Nevertheless, Eve is in love and love knows no refusals. She allows herself to be pushed on the bed and she allows the red shirt to be ripped from her shoulders, the belt to be unbuckled, and with some difficulty she allows the hip-huggers to be tugged over her ass and ankles and feet. He reaches between her legs to assure himself of her lubrication and then, remarkably, leaps from the bed, his erection at a 45-degree angle, and switches on the TV. It's an announcer with a loud voice and a group of female contestants in green spandex, perhaps triplets. They are talking about shampoo, Eve thinks, but Tingo is on top of her, pushing himself inside and finishing up almost simultaneously, so it's hard to hear. This isn't how I imagined it, says Eve. For an instant he rests the side of his cheek on her shoulder and takes two deep, impatient sounding breaths. Then he rises from the bed and switches off the TV. It's noon, he informs Eve coldly. I need to go.

Who cares that he was a lousy lover? Who cares that a woman with blonde hair down to her ass visits him during lunch hour and they sit in a corner of the courtyard laughing and feeding each other bites of torta. Who cares?

7

Eve is obsessed but she is intelligent enough to recognize obsession for what it is. That it has less to do with the man himself than it has to do with her primal needs for unconditional love, which were never met. She watches her obsession, its forward and backward action, its clenching and melodrama, as one might watch a baseball game. After a while it begins to pale.

She begins to act decently to Miracula and Frank, only she doesn't really love Frank anymore. She plans to break their engagement but, in the meantime, she is cordial, although she refuses to have sex. Lily, who is madly in love with a 21-year-old homosexual sculptor, lies around the house without any energy since she refuses to eat. She is so thin that when she is stretched on the sofa, Miracula, Eve, and Frank can sit comfortably alongside one another, and, if not for the scraggly blanket she has wrapped around her legs, would not realize there was a person there at all. This is a great lesson to Eve who vows to keep her emotions in check from now on. All thoughts of revolution have left her mind and she fervently hopes that the guerillas will not enter the city to cause further havoc in her life or in the lives of her loved ones.
The End.

or

Eve is obsessed and her obsession takes her into the unsavory reaches of her imagination. She has taken to committing little vindictive acts of retaliation—tearing up Tingo's worksheets, spilling water on his Rolodex, calling him on the phone and then hanging up. She waits outside his house in a clump of bushes and watches the stream of women who enter enthusiastically and leave sadly. This should alert her to the fact that Tingo is not worth the trouble, but in fact it increases her love for him.

Finally, she is making her own revolution. What need does she have of an army?

At home she refuses to speak to Miracula, who is flummoxed at her own behavior being turned against her, and she tells Frank she never wants to see him again. She lies next to Lily at the other end of the green sofa and starves herself, so that between Eve and Lily there is hardly anyone on the sofa at all. After a while she dies of love and the exhaustion of battle and Lily dies two days later.
The End.

or

Eve is obsessed and she decides to cut her hair. She feels in some way she can't quite put her finger on that cutting her hair is a remedy for obsession. Perhaps once who she has become is destroyed, the pain of her life will miraculously disappear. Or perhaps a haircut will give her a fresh start on life and a whole new Eve will emerge, free from obsession and guilt and shame and terror at being left alone forever, and self-pity. The only trouble is, she can't seem to decide on a style: a bob, a French, a Caesar, a twirl, a spiral, layered or blunt. She decides to leave it up to God and her beautician.

Eve goes to the beauty hairdresser wearing a backless green dress, matching pantyhose, black pumps, and silver earrings. The peluquera, whose name is Marty, tells her to relax and look at her knees. In the corner of her eye she keeps track of the hair piling up, layer upon layer of it, dark with little gray ripples, tangles and knots and curls. I feel like I'm walking on a rug, says Marty. When Eve finally looks at herself in the mirror she is amazed to find an attractive short-haired woman. What a nice face, she thinks. She is cheerful as she leaves, weightless and reborn.

Miracula says, At last I can see your nice ears!

Two weeks later, however, she begins to miss her hair. Her face looks too big, her neck too long and scrawny, she feels as though she's lost all her sex appeal. More crucially, she can no longer hide her face and peer out from underneath. She is finding she has to reconceptualize not only herself but the world, to adopt a straightforward approach, to abandon irony and evasiveness because nothing anymore is uncertain; the world, which had formerly been complex and vague, stings her eyes with its color and pain and terrible edges.

Marry me, Frank, she says one night on impulse. Maybe she is trying to prove herself, maybe she is desperate. Sure, says Frank, he's picking his teeth with a fork. Sure baby, he says. Lately his job has kept him busy until all hours.

Now she is on the green sofa with Lily and they are sharing a cheese sandwich. Love is hell, Lily says. Men are such imbeciles, so necessary, so misogynist. They drive us mad, Eve agrees. They turn us into bitches and whores. Yes, says Lily. Outside the birds are singing raucously, and there is the clatter of the best burrito place in town folding up for the day. History, Eve says, if we could only understand it, if we could only grasp it in all its shapelessness and chaos. Yes, says Lily, I think it's because it needs an ending to put it into perspective.

The End.
or

When Eve and Lily go off to join the revolution, they are wearing Eve's father's old army fatigues, tee shirts, jean jackets, and, slung over their shoulders, a rifle each. They carry rucksacks with notebooks and sandwiches. From here you can see them making their way up the long hill that leads out of the city and in the direction of the mountain camp of the guerillas. They link arms, Eve and Lily. They are two dots on a landscape that is otherwise unblemished and serene. Soon they will vanish altogether over the crest of the hill, leaving only the brushed dirt of their footprints and the ambiguous scent of their perfume.

Estrella inhumanas.
Pero la hora nuestra.
Octavio Paz

MAYA SUE

THAT TIME, SHE WAS saying, I wore fishnet stockings to my eighth grade prom they kicked me out, this weird couple who were called upon to chaperone and they wouldn't ever of course refuse because of their dorky son Robert Hasa who had no eyebrows already swear to God balding at the age eleven and they kicked me out because I looked like a slut so I went to Central Park with my boyfriend, we met these beautiful Puerto Rican junkies sitting near the fishpond and the most beautiful had a gun tucked in the waistband of his jeans, swear to God it reminded me of a penis and that was the first time I shot up.

All I can tell you about it is that it was GREAT.

So I moved in with my new boyfriend Miguel only we called him Mike and he was gorgeous, black eyes and hair and a great butt smaller than mine and kinky, he'd wear my underpants when he washed the dishes, didn't care about anything, all that macho shit, he liked my underpants so why not? Only my parents never knew about Mike they'd freak out, my mother's a producer and my father teaches history at Columbia, he's so cute, he's always saying, Are you mescing Maya Sue? because the only drugs he approves of are mota and mescaline, he'd freak out if he knew about anything else, but it's all part of growing up which I know is important to him, I mean I know he wants me to have experiences which is why we're any of us here right?

I love this day, I love you guys, I've been thinking about history, how it's all bullshit, all historians do is invent stuff and also because my name is historical, Maya Sue, Maya after the Mayans, a highly civilized and amazingly developed early empire that flourished from fifteen-hundred B.C. to about three-hundred B.C. I'm great at dates, it's great being named after an empire, the Sue part is after my sweet grandmother who I love so much but who is now senile and goes around wearing her bra over her ears and eating out of the cat box and shit like that.

I love history and I love horses, two things, when I was eight I rode a horse over those hills right there with my parents which was freaky because I thought the guide was holding the lead but wasn't and the horse galloped off and there I was having to learn to ride without any instruction, and the horse was so cool a chestnut mare with those amazing eyes and after a while she calmed down it was like we were in perfect sync with each other riding over the hills I thought well I've come this far I may as well keep going but after a while my parents caught up and my mom was crying.

I'd die to ride a horse right now but I'm too fucked up, I'd probably kill myself.

I almost killed myself after Mike left, I thought about it once or twice, I thought maybe I'd just do an overdose but it's a bad way to go though you wouldn't think so, then I thought I'd put a gun to my mouth and pull the trigger, I know this guy who did that in front of his girlfriend and she was freaked out for months after, then I got sick of thinking about dying you know I'm basically a life loving person, it's just the way I am.

Mike was great but he was you know violent, everything about him cruising for a showdown, in bars he'd come unglued if a guy touched me even by accident like on the way to the restroom and there'd be Mike with that stupid gun aiming but not shooting, he never actually shot anyone.

Come to think of it that was the bad part about him, all talk, said we'd go to California, did we ever go to Brooklyn? We never swear to God went to New Jersey.

All talk.

I was fourteen and he was twenty five, he had a great business, highly successful, careful about who copped but the money don't ask me about the money.

Don't ask me about Mike who frankly bums me out in retrospect because and in this way he's like my parents all talk and no delivery.

Did I tell you my mom's a producer and she is so beautiful men go nuts over her, she does exactly what she wants, we're alike in that way, she knows everyone, Jerry Seinfeld, Sarah Silverman, once I came home and there was Jerry Seinfeld swear to God in the living room drinking a beer, Hi I said, what're you going to say to Seinfeld? But it was so cool, I went to my room and did two lines I was so nervous and then I was a great conversationalist.

Jerry said to my mom, Maya Sue is very lively and intelligent, which is true even without coke. I was first in my ninth grade class until I got kicked out and my best subject was you guessed it history even though I don't believe in it. We had a teacher who used to say history teaches what history preaches or the other way around or some shit. The guy was a moron, head like a Crenshaw melon and practically blind, a huge body, we used to call him Brontosaurus Man, still I got all A's. Dig this: the Spanish Conquest was fifteen twenty-one and independence from Spain came exactly three-hundred years later in eighteen twenty-one. I hated that fucker Cortés, he used to burn people's feet.

I wish I didn't start talking about Mike, it bums me out, I had to kick junk after he left because what am I going to do, say Hey Dad I've got this little minor jones I need help with? And I wasn't into tricking, too dangerous. I had a friend Emma who got beat up, a concussion, three broken ribs, she was sixteen and gorgeous then she got mean looking, you can tell a whore by her eyes they say which is true because after the beating Emma's real eyes disappeared and the replacements had no kindness in them.

Sometimes I wish I would burn up. No, excuse me, sometimes I am burning up. I'm on fire and I'm riding a horse or I'm running or fucking someone hard, on top. I think I exist for explosions, it's my sign Aries.

My father's a Scorpio, my mom's an Aries like me, she doesn't take shit from anyone, sometimes I hear her in her office screaming at Jimmy Kimmel on the phone, Fuck you Jimmy, I need it yesterday, asshole. I love my mother, I love my father better, I loved Miguel more than anyone until he moved to Watts with this skaggy girl from the West Bronx— I couldn't believe she was such a pig— and got arrested.

I love that boy group from a million years ago especially that cool line about sticking his dick in mashed potatoes and I love you guys and this dope isn't bad either. I want a vodka though. I'm getting old.

I want to go to an art museum and cop in the rest room with my friend Sally which we actually did once at the Met and then we spent hours on different floors getting these like profound insights about Impressionism and Picasso and shit. Do you know that painting Guernica by Picasso? It's so cool, it's my favorite painting, it's all about the war and violence and humanity and culture, it's mucho profound. He was so brilliant, Picasso, only he was a dick to women. Did you know that? I hate this chair, it's leaving little slat lines on my butt.

Do you know Jack Kerouac? Do you know Grace Paley? She came over once ages ago, before I was born, but Jack Kerouac's an asshole, my granddad used to hang out with him. Do you guys want more weed? I'm broke but I love it down here, I'd live down here full time because it's oh like one big day and night, one big day with sun and rain and shit and shopping and eating delicious, superb, out of sight food like enchiladas and al pastors and then at night going to Mia's and Pops and Pancho's and then back to Mia's again. Know what? I never pay for shit, I just walk out, they don't care, it blows me away, in the States they'd have my ass in jail or they'd call my parents, but here I guess it's the mañana mentality and I'm the benefactor or benefactress, how do you say that?

Did I tell you I was beaten up the other night? You should see me naked, I call myself Battered Barbie, bruises like stained glass windows, Mom says. Were you ever in Chartres? Notre Dame? Does anyone have anything—pot? vodka? I could do with some c but I'm too broke, swear to God I'd blow someone for a line of coke I feel so like needy these days, and all I did was spit on the guy's shoes cause he was insulting me, and he decks me and I claw his face, swear to God there was skin under my nails and then everyone beat on the guy, and he was banned from the bar forever, so it turned out cool. It's typical of these guys, the way they treat women, I hate to be racist though, I wasn't raised that way. Fuck I lived with a Puerto Rican and I can't tell you how many black guys I've been in love with.

God, I wish I had my good clothes here, I'd blow this town away. I have these platforms a foot swear to God high, silver with iron spokes in them, like Gaga, and I have a dress made out of hard black plastic, my boobs look great in it, that doesn't fit in my closet.

I wish I had a dog though, I like animals and they like me, a dog would be great, I'd name him Ernest after Hemingway, and he'd get to know all those other poor sorry stray dogs in town. When I leave I'm going to buy a case of Alpo and just hand it out, it's so sad, the quality of civilization makes me incredibly sad.

I've thought a lot about how we're supposed to be civilized and everyone, even me, goes around piercing body parts. What is that? I have, let's see, eleven body piercings and three in very private places, one through my clit which I recommend by the way.

Is that a parade? There's always a parade here, they're so boring marching up and down, and the music sucks. I wish I could sing. I'd sing *Maya Maya Maya Sue Sue Sue.* I'd sing a song to myself.

GHOSTS

A RECIPE FOR ENCHILADA sauce might involve soaking the chiles in boiling water for five minutes, slicing them in strips, tossing them in the blender with a few cloves of garlic, salt, and stock. The blender is an old Osterizer with a glass container and as it accelerates into high gear, pureeing the chiles until they are the color of Raquel's dress, not a dark or a bright red, but soft as skin, we think we see something out of the corner of our eye. We are listening to the whirring of the blender which blots out all sound: birds, water splashing in the big tiled tubs, the clang clang of the garbage truck men who beat the sides of the truck with rods as if they were in a salsa band. Then there is the quick flash we have become accustomed to: a fleeting movement off to the side which rounds the edge of the dish cabinet. A heart could stop in the space of this movement, but if you're steady you pretend you don't see. This is the great trick of the underworld, but it didn't work for Gordon and it didn't work for Rojelio.

We have been warned not to go to a certain café which is where Gordon meets his drug dealing friends. This café with its black and white tiles, its television room in the back, its herd of piñatas suspended from the ceiling with green string, nevertheless attracts us. We go there for a game of pool at one of the big tables in the back or we go for fajitas and before we know it we know more than we want to. We are sitting in the back room, adjacent to the pool tables, clustered around a tiny TV. Gordon is the one with his back to us. He is a tall, blond man from LA who wears a gold chain flamboyantly around his neck, who leaves the buttons of his shirt undone to the waist, whose chest is covered with blond fur, like a cat's. He is a sculptor, who is famous (more or less) for these tiny plaster of Paris figurines of young women. We all know this about Gordon, that he likes young women, and we are repulsed by this fact, but what can we do? Once in a while, Gordon gets lucky and this returns us to that which we have tried to forget. He is walking with a young chiquita, her hair swinging loose in a pony tail, her lipstick dark red; or with a blue-eyed Americana with muscles like naranjas who is too stupid to know Gordon's game. His game is this: promises. To the chiquita a movie star contract, to the gringa, drugs. Either way, they undress in Gordon's studio and they parade for him on the patio with a 360-degree view of the city. They are artists' models, they are future movie stars, their diminutive breasts have just begun to form, and Gordon tells them they are remarkable. Gordon's sculptures are not, however, remarkable. He is at best a mediocre craftsman and, at worst, a creator of crass, sentimentalized eyesores. He has trouble selling his work on its own merits, but he uses the hollows at the base of each piece—which is to say, at the base of each replica of each young girl he seduces—to smuggle cocaine and heroin into the States.

Everyone knows this about Gordon, and everyone turns a blind eye. We are in his proximity at the popular café, clustered around TV at the NBA playoffs, and he makes us shudder. Gordon is an ebullient Knicks fan, buying a round of tequila shots for every 3-point goal. There is nothing about Gordon we like or admire but because we want to root for our team, which is the opposing team, we are in his proximity, the hairs on our arms raising. The other reason we are here is that the once-charming array of sounds in this city have made us suddenly nervous—the clangs and squawks and parades and splashing water and the footsteps echoing on the cobblestones down the whole length of the street—and here in the café we have found a way to stifle, if only for an hour or two, this incessant humanity and to plant ourselves dumbly in front of the TV screen. Plus, we use the telephone in the back room to call our friends back home and occasionally order hamburgers.

Now Rojelio is a different breed of thug. He wears suits, expensive and tasteful ties, he carries a briefcase of the finest Italian leather, and he would not be caught dead in the café where the North Americanos go. If he wants the NBA playoffs, he watches them from the privacy of his solarium, perched high over the city, his home like an elaborate bird's nest, the satellite dish tilted elegantly in the night skies, as if to catch an entire constellation. His wife who is thin and adorable with little curlicues of hair adorning her forehead, sits by his side. His son picks his teeth with a pencil. We never see Rojelio up close, only in a blur as he whisks past; only through the large many-paned window of his solarium is he clearly though distantly visible, his stockinged feet stretched luxuriously in front of him, on the tufted ottoman, his large hands encircling the pretty neck of his wife. He is also a Knicks fan, but he watches with a closed face, with eyes that are intelligent but cynical. When the point guard misses a 3-pointer, there is no discernible crease on his brow, even though he has twenty thousand riding on the game.

Rojelio is Gordon's boss, even a fool could figure this out. They meet in El Jardin in the evenings and sit on one of the green metal benches under the big trees and there they negotiate, though it would be truer to say that Rojelio barks out orders and Gordon grovels. Rojelio despises Gordon. He despises his tastelessness, his proclivity for children, his stupidity. He cannot even bring himself to admire the one quality of Gordon's which makes him indispensable—which is an uncanny cool in the face of tremendous adversity. It is Gordon who manages, with his hearty, superficially clever manner, his blond hair slopped over to one side, to talk the customs official out of a full search of the wooden crates transporting the figurines to Arizona. He hands the seductive statuettes of young girls around like a munificent Santa—these of course from a clean create, marked boldly with an X for these purposes. Without Gordon, Rojelio's network is diminished. And without Rojelio, Gordon is dead. He knows this and most of us know this as well. Though, as usual, we'd prefer not to know. There are things we prefer not to know but they come upon anyway, unbidden, like a flash of light or darkness at the periphery of our vision.

Ghosts, says Raquel, who is famous for her sensitivity to such phenomenon, who sees the pink aura around a globe of eggplant and predicts rain for the next day. The ghosts are everywhere. There is something primitive, isn't there, about the way we warm the tortillas on the burner of the stove and if, as Raquel says, the ghosts are nearby they must be pleased with how we are making these enchiladas—according to tradition, that is, so as not to disturb anything. Ghosts, if there are such things, want everything to remain the way it was. This is what brings them the most comfort: to sense that nothing is out of place, that the old ways continue. Thus, they are able to stay joined to life, which thrills them.

In the café, during halftime, Gordon converses with two men, North Americans, both wearing LA Dodgers caps and jeans, both short and dumpy and boisterous. They sit in a corner of the room, over behind the pool tables and they talk in modulated voices. At one point, Gordon retrieves a small bent notebook from the hip pocket of his jeans and writes something in it. One of the men puts on reading glasses. A waiter serves them bottles of beer with a little saucer of cut-up limes. We are not meant to hear what negotiations transpire between the three men, but we can imagine. Every once in a while, Gordon laughs loudly, and the others follow suit with their even more strident laughter. Then halftime is over, and they stroll leisurely to the TV, where they cheer loudly and obnoxiously for the team we are rooting against.

Rojelio, on the other hand, switches off the set at halftime and does not plan to turn it on again. Watching the game has made him restless. He would simply like the results, not all the irritating fanfare leading up to the final score. Actually, he does not care for this kind of game. It seems to him infantile, grown men throwing a ball into a net and shoving and hitting each other in the process. Primitive. He switches on the light in his library and looks with pleasure at his long row of bookcases, at the colorful and expensive spines of his books. He randomly selects a volume of Plato's dialogues and reads: *So it seems absurd to me that, as long as I am in ignorance of myself, I should concern myself with extraneous matters. Therefore I let all such things be as they may, and think not of them but of myself.* Thus, he satisfies himself with the wisdom of the Greeks. When his wife enters the room in her white nightgown, he claps the book shut, shakes his head with a preoccupied frown and waves her away. At his desk he opens a fat ledger, gray and official looking, and begins his calculations. Outside the Parroquia bells are ringing and as he lifts his head to gaze for a moment toward the window, in the night skies he sees a white bat soar by, its body as big as a gull's.

We see the bat as well, huge and tremorous, winding through the air. There are caves all around the city, in the small grayish cliffs and in the fissures between boulders and sometimes unexpectedly, on the side of a metal shed or an abandoned wooden shack in the hills. These are huge bats called murcielago and Raquel says they are the opposite of angels. Now they are carving up the night sky, presiding over the span of the dreaming city, we shudder, even though they are beautiful, amazing creatures. Be careful, Raquel warns us. Because for her everything has a meaning in addition to the fact of itself. Whether we are leaving the café or here at home, making enchiladas and happening to look up. Tonight, that bat is everywhere, crisscrossing the city in huge loops, and the ghosts are dashing incessantly behind our backs—we feel the cold wind of them as they go and we believe, as Raquel says, that something will happen.

What may happen is this: At midnight two men get out of a long bronze car and go with iron rods to the house of Gordon, who is at this point raping a fourteen-year-old girl. The men enter Gordon's house with care, sliding a flat device into the lock and lifting it quietly, though there is really no great need for caution since Gordon is preoccupied and also drunk. The girl is a virgin and she is at this point staring at the ceiling in a fixed way and praying to the Mother of God to forgive her. While Gordon thrusts inside of her, his face mashed into the pillow, intent only on his own fulfillment, the thrill of ravaging the small body beneath him, she hears the footsteps and she hears the door to the room opening and in her heart she thanks the Mother of God for this fortuitous interruption. Then she is looking into the face of a man who is raising his iron rod and breaking open Gordon's head.

At Rojelio's house there is not much drama. A clean shot above the ear right through the library window. Bullseye. His wife finds him in a pool of blood and leaves the room. It's because the man on the carpet is no longer my husband, she will explain to friends.

We may read about it in the papers the next day and we would marvel, the way one does, at the coincidence of seeing Gordon just hours before at the café, as alive as any of us, knocking back shots of tequila and licking the salt from his fist. We hated Gordon, and Rojelio scared us. Instead of grieving for their deaths we are relieved that we are unscathed, perfect and whole and alive, and we go to the terrace and breathe the air deeply, filling our lungs; and the air seems sweeter than usual and the sounds of the squawking birds and the clanking trucks make us smile.

And as we continue our cooking, chopping cilantro for the garnish, crumbling cheese into the palms of tortillas and rolling them up, we feel a prickle come over our skin and a finger move in our hair. Soon, there is a noise coming from the carved wardrobe, a little rustling among the clothes. But perhaps we are bound to see ghosts when we make enchiladas, the way we make them. Hopefully not Gordon and Rojelio hiding in the wardrobe, resisting the afterlife (unless they're sitting on a green bench in El Jardin, Rojelio growling out orders and Gordon looking sheepishly at his knees). Raquel in her red dress sweeps around our feet and chuckles softly to herself. She knows things before they happen because she is skilled at reading signs which to most of us are obscure. She tells us that everything has a future which it owns completely and once that future is past things get confused. When the sauce bubbles around the tortillas and the cheese softens without browning, at exactly that moment, we must turn off the oven. Otherwise, she tells us, what will happen will not be what we expect.

THE RED ROOM

CAROLINE HAS NO IDEA who she is anymore and so she is willing to surrender to the city. Living here, she feels, is like living in a different element. Like water, leagues beneath the sea, among alien slow-moving creatures and vegetation that seems strangely alive and ominous. And time is affected too, moving dreamily in lethargic passages or over-abruptly, as if a large chunk of events had been passed over, or some logical transition artfully evaded.

When it rains, the strangeness is accentuated, and as she races along the stone sidewalks or slips over the old cobbles which tear up her Italian espadrilles, fat streams of water pour from the brass mouths of fish high on the walls of the buildings, and in the distance the light is blurry and ethereal as if preparing for an apparition.

Is this city dreaming itself or are we dreaming the city? she asks herself. Is the image in the eye of the beholder as we were taught to believe, or elsewhere, in the way light shapes itself around a doorway or a tree?

Caroline is changing. More specifically, her heart which had once been full of love for a particular man, a man she married and lived with for many years and eventually left, is changing. She has come to the city to recuperate, therefore, to try to discover a way to accept her life because she is aging, and it seems to her the time has come for acceptance. Chances are, she will never marry again. Though it horrifies her to think so, she may never make love again. She walks in the rain, head crunched into her chest, a kind of rueful sadness welling up in her, not unmixed with self-pity.

Then, as quickly as it began twenty minutes ago, with a low rumble in a bank of eggplant-colored clouds, the rain stops and the night air takes on a deep many-faceted clarity, and an extraordinary stillness enfolds the street, almost a paralysis. Only Caroline—for the street happens to be empty—is in motion, striding ahead with purpose, though in the dreamy light her purpose gradually wavers and she begins to walk more slowly and reflectively.

Her life with her husband had been unhappy. He had been selfish and self-absorbed. Eventually she'd felt, after years of abnegation, she was losing whatever spark had always ignited her being and kept her going; this is what terrified her and caused her to leave him. By vocation, she is a photographer and she believes passionately in the vision of the artist, in the ability of artists to recreate themselves in their art, a belief she counts on to save her from herself and her terror.

To this city she has brought her cameras and a few photographic supplies and she spends a good part of each day wandering about in search of images that trigger a sense of recognition in her—the familiar in the unfamiliar, whatever can return her to herself. This is more difficult than one would expect: To sit in the park and to watch, as she did this afternoon, the washerwomen laboring over the long tiled tubs with their black plastic bags of laundry is to witness how this culture resists the spectator—with clichés—and how the clichés themselves—the washerwomen, the beggar children, the old men with their burros and their sacks of corn—have made the culture curiously impenetrable to the tourist. For what we want,

Caroline acknowledges with shame, is to penetrate, to own, to exploit. We are imperialists in our souls.

Now a dog howls briefly, a sound halfway between a yawn and a whimper, and Caroline sees something. A flicker in her peripheral vision which, like a star's distant light, registered after the fact, causes her to stop and retrace her steps. There, emanating from a voluptuous space between two heavy beige drapes is a rose-tinted glow, a shaft of light that pours onto the stones of the sidewalk and continues across the narrow street and up the façade of the opposite building, continuing on, supernaturally, as if it will never end.

The source of the light is a goose-necked lamp in a small, impeccably tidy room. The lamp light, which is modest enough in itself, has apparently picked up the cast of the flocked wine-red upholstery on the two chairs and on the matching sofa. These are arranged in a cozy grouping, the chairs opposing the sofa and positioned on a Persian rug. In the center of the rug is a glass-topped table on which reside several tiny figurines—perhaps of animals—and a large vase of red roses, their stems crushed together but their blooms at the peak of freshness, velvety, intricate, gracefully arched.

But the focal point of the space between the beige drapes, within the warm glow cast by the wine-red upholstery and the roses, is a small marble fireplace. On the mantel, slanted against the wall, is an enlarged sepia-colored photograph of a boy with dark eyebrows and a wistful expression on his face. This is what holds Caroline's attention, the face of the boy, the provocative placement of the photograph in her direct line of vision. He is wearing a batiste lace collar around his thin neck and that, as well as the coloring of the photograph, marks it as from another, long ago era. Also on the mantel, a circle of votive candles glimmer faintly in glass cups, and these cast flickers of light on the photo of the boy, and seem to have been lit out of deference to him.

Caroline stands a while—too long—in front of the window, gazing between the drapes, taking inventory. She wishes she had her camera with her, she hadn't expected to find an image so perfect and so impossible. But what would it be to look into a window and take a photograph without their permission?

Nevertheless, she is riveted to the spot, she can't help staring and wondering. What attracts her to this room is that it seems both intensely private and at the same time to be arranged for the benefit of the spectator—herself—with the curtains enticingly parted just wide enough to frame a harmonious though oddly chilling setting; likewise, the photograph of the boy reveals only so much, enough to set the imagination in flight.

Love is what comes to Caroline's mind. The room has been tenderly, meticulously tended with love. Which reminds her of her house with her husband, the living room with its spider plants and pale dhurrie rug, the oak rocking chair he gave her for a birthday. In the evenings they'd watch TV in this room, sprawled on either end of the white sofa, their feet touching under the mohair blanket. On one set of shelves were his collection of bowls, mostly South American and American Indian and in another were her books, Dickens, George Eliot, Jane Austen. She had thought they would grow old together, him and her, in this room, watching TV, chatting between shows or arguing or kissing. But she had felt oppressed by him, his overwhelming need for her, his depression, his workaholicism. She had made the right decision for herself and yet she missed him. This was the simple truth of the matter. Because without him, who was she? Not the long-suffering wife and not the optimistic woman either, the one who assured them both that life would turn out for the best.

Now, looking at the photograph of the boy with the dark eyebrows, it comes to her that the whole purpose of the room is to pay tribute to this boy, and it comes to her that the room is therefore a mausoleum, a monument to a dead boy. The idea makes her shudder and as she looks into the wistful expression of the boy, a boy no longer alive but commemorated and mourned for, the face of her husband superimposes itself over the boy's face and the room becomes her living room with the dhurrie rug and the oak rocker.

Suddenly he is there, now moving to the white sofa with his newspaper and a plate of pasta on a tray on his lap and he is staring gravely at the newspaper, in his characteristic way, running his eyes down the columns, and shoving in forkfuls of pasta as he reads. David, she wants to cry out. But instead he smiles when a woman, not her, appears in a pink bathrobe holding a book and a glass of milk. Ready for bed? says the woman. And David rises from the couch, folding his newspaper under one arm and with the other encircling the woman's waist, they leave the room.

How unfair, thinks Caroline, that he should be the one to find some-one. He who loved me so imperfectly, who made me so miserable! And something twists in her heart, thinking of him with the woman in the pink bathrobe and of herself alone, living her solitary life.

Then the boy with the dark eyebrows resumes his place in the photo-graph, the little votives glimmering around him as if they will last forever. It seems to her that no one tends this room, that no one enters or leaves or sweeps or polishes or arranges the tall velvety roses in the glass vase. No one will ever recline on the sofa, no one will ever converse with another on the two chairs; the fireplace will never be lit, nor will a cat come to curl and sleep on the hearth. Likewise, the boy's eyes, forever wistful, will haunt her as she makes her way over the slippery cobbles into whatever comes next.

ART AND DEATH

NOW PEOPLE ARE RUSHING through the great arches of the Instituto, wearing Guatemalan scarves and Chiapas blouses and heavy silver jewelry purchased from the antique shops or from David's Joyeria. Swinging into the tide of them she goes, up the long staircase and into the courtyard which has been set up with punch bowls and plastic cups and which gives out onto three galleries. In the corner by the entrance to one of these Elizabeth is talking to a man, attractive, Caroline decides as she comes closer, not very tall, balding, well-dressed.

Caroline! says Elizabeth. I've been describing you to Max. What do you think, Max? Did I do a good job or what? Isn't she sweet? I love your dress, look at this dress, my God it's perfect! She touches the neck of Caroline's dress, which is an old dress, fifteen years or so old, which even then had been purchased at a thrift shop. Simple elegance is what I said, exactly my words to Max. Verify for me Max, will you? Max smiles. A pleasure, he says. Nice dress.

Together they enter one of the galleries, going from painting to painting, squinting at the descriptions beneath, the prices. In retrospect Caroline will remember two of these paintings: one of terra cotta and black horses, a large canvas and the horses sketched in impressionistically, and another more realistically rendered of men in a swimming pool, only their heads are visible, it seems like heads rolling in some kind of soup. She especially likes this one. The colors are luminous, the way you'd expect Renaissance frescos colors to have been before they faded.

I like that one too, says Max. I like a painting that makes me feel like a spectator. It seems more honest to acknowledge one's voyeurism. Rather than? says Caroline. Max shrugs. Rather than pretending we don't like to look. And with this he examines her, pleasantly, she realizes, even though it gives her an unpleasant feeling.

Max himself is an artist, says Elizabeth. Then she offers to take their empty cups and refill them, and as she hurries off her limp seems more pronounced than usual, her left foot seeming to jerk a little which makes her body crooked.

It's a pity, says Max. What's a pity? says Caroline, because she feels disloyal discussing her friend with this relative stranger. But all he says is: Perhaps you're right. Perhaps we waste our sympathies on those who are just fine. Her life could not be otherwise, he adds, which is what makes her so remarkable. You feel that in certain people, that they have claimed their lives.

He takes her arm. You, for example, are the opposite of Elizabeth— enchanting, a bit unstable, perhaps enchanting because a bit unstable. Nature abhors completion.

I thought it was a vacuum that Nature abhorred, says Caroline, and she feels she's put just the right amount of edge to her voice and that she'd conveyed her insult and his presumption, because he releases her arm then and turns to talk to a woman wearing a turban, leaning in to kiss this woman and touch her shoulder.

God, she says to Elizabeth when she returns with their refilled cups.

Who is that guy? Max? she says. Oh, he's been around for years. Once he murdered a man so we all call him Max the Murderer. Even to his face? asks Caroline? No, not to his face, says Elizabeth.

———

Max had been in love with Emma. This was years ago, before many people were here and so all the people who were here knew each other very well. There is something always about being in a foreign country and finding one's countrymen—even those you would normally abhor seem familiar and therefore likeable. This, at any rate, was the way it was then—before cappuccino machines and Italian restaurants.

We used to go, Elizabeth continued, to this one bar called Chelo's and drink rum and play cards. It was like the way the Wild West must have been. We were all a little lost and a little frightened and yet we told ourselves and each other what a great adventure it was to be living here. To have had the courage to move here. To the horror, of course, of our families back home who imagined us huddling in lean-tos in a jungle full of hostile natives and contaminated food.

Emma, who Max loved, was married to Robert Sanders, who was probably the only one of us with any credibility. He was very wealthy. Also, he was a writer who had published twenty-one short stories. He used to tell people that whenever he got the chance, and so we took to calling him Robert "Twenty-One Short Stories" Sanders. Who knew where he got them published? But in those days, we didn't care. It was enough that he had done something, however humble, in what we referred to as the Real World, and by some curious logic all of our flights to Mexico were sanctified by his.

Emma was an incredibly delicate woman, short, fair, and shy. Of the two of them it was Robert who did the talking. Emma sat in a corner of Chelo's with her cigarette looking nervous and cold. I can see her still with a thin pale blue sweater wrapped around her shoulders, smoking a cigarette—she rolled her own—while her husband, big, blond and opinionated in a way that sucked the oxygen out of the room, held forth, usually on himself and more specifically on the pain of being an artist in today's world, which was fucked, according to him, and doomed.

Despite his size, there was something dandy-ish about Robert. He wore dark glasses and styled himself rather self-consciously. He was moody, too. Rumor had it he knocked Emma around. Once he threw a chair against a wall and it splintered, like in the movies. A chunk of wood caught our friend Marco's ear and he had to have stitches. Another time he handed around copies of a manuscript of poems for our comments. We had nothing better to do and Robert was our entertainment. In some ways, he was our leader.

And it was darker then than it is now. How can I explain it? There were so few of us. The quality of light was different. Also, we were all a little lost. So, Robert assumed the position of leadership among us. We didn't like him much, but we respected his energy. Most of us, including Emma, even including Max, were too confused to contest his authority.

Max was a fugitive from the law. We all knew that, but he wasn't a murderer yet. He had done something—we never found out what—we liked to imagine he'd robbed a bank. We liked to imagine grandiose pasts for each other, it gave us dignity. Max was handsome and intense. He had a tough appeal, but it was not the appeal that comes from brute physicality, like Robert; Max was, as he is now, wiry, contained. He spoke softly. Sometimes you had to lean in to hear him.

He arrived on our scene a few months after Robert and Emma came. Right away, you could see the sexual tension between Emma and Max. Though they never spoke, even at Chelo's they never sat near one another. I used to watch them avoiding each other's eyes. That avoidance gave us thrills.

The affair began the day Max came to Emma's with roses. He'd purchased these astonishing roses from a woman who used to sell them door-to-door. They had heads the size of grapefruits and they were all colors—peach, yellow, white, pink. The roses in his arms looked incongruous to Emma, as if someone had thrown them to him as a joke. He was standing in the middle of the courtyard and the light fell over his shoulder and shone directly on the roses, as in a painting.

I thought I'd bring these by, was all he said. Emma was agitated. Her hair was pulled up, untidy. She wore an old shirt of Robert's that was covered with paint. Barefoot. In retrospect, I suppose she looked charming. But at the time it made her self-conscious. She wasn't an extrovert to begin with and Max's arrival with the roses, so unexpected, rendered her speechless.

She took the roses from him and turned to walk to the kitchen. Max followed. She removed the long shears from the hook above the sink and spread the roses on the blue and yellow tiled counter. One by one, she clipped the extra leaves and the stems. Her hands trembled. At one point, Max sighed behind her.

That was the only sound in the room for quite a while—that sigh of Max's which dismayed Emma. She was not sure what it indicated. Impatience with her? Finally, she forced herself to say, These are beautiful.

Then he took her in his arms. She began to tremble uncontrollably. It's ok, he said. It's ok, dear, he said.

And that was how it began, with the roses on the tiled counter and Emma in Max's arms. Emma had never known anything like it. She had been a sheltered woman, a girl actually, until Robert came along when she was in college. He was her first boyfriend, he had a trust fund, and she married him. She had been passionate about him, but she never understood him. Max she felt she understood. His dark moods mirrored her own. Everything about Robert was geared to the outside world, whereas Max and Emma were turned inward, like certain flowers.

They met during the day. He lived above an apothecary and his apartment always smelled of dying plants. It was a potent, nostalgic smell. It reminded her of autumn.

They made love on his mattress, under an old army blanket. Oh it was so typical, a cliché! Under an army blanket, green of course, with Max's German shepherd lolling nearby. He kept a gun on a table near the mattress. Once Emma put it in her mouth during sex, she was feeling wild, as if the world could end any minute. It excited Max tremendously, but he never asked her to do it again. He never asked her for anything.

It seemed to Emma that they didn't need words. It seemed to her that they understood each other without talking, without exchanging thoughts or philosophies. Their thoughts were one, she felt.

Yet, and here's the quandary, she loved Robert too. Robert pulled her out of herself, forced her to confront the world. It was Robert who pointed out the goats grazing on the side of the mountain with their little beards which seemed to float just ahead of them, the white bats who flooded the city at twilight in certain seasons. It was Robert who read the newspapers, who kept in touch, who argued in Chelo's, who urged, privately, her own self-expression. Her opinions were foreign to him, but they were interesting. He told her this on many occasions: You are interesting, Emma, you have an original mind, Emma. Max was her twin, her soulmate, but Robert kept her pinned to the earth.

She never wanted him to find out about Max. But you can't keep a secret in a small town and too many people disliked Robert to protect him from pain. He went straight to Max's to confront him. You're a son-of-a-bitch, he told him. At which point Max shot him. The gun was so handy. He shot him and wrapped him in the army blanket and dragged him to the street and loaded him into the trunk of the car. His plan was to drive to the desert surrounding the city and deposit him. He didn't have a shovel and a burial was out of the question.

It was raining and the roads were slippery and Max drove recklessly. The car slid over a cliff and landed in a garbage dump. There was trash everywhere, blowing in what was by now a full-fledged storm, and the sounds of bottles and tin cans smashing against one another.

The first thing he did was open the trunk. Robert stared at him, wild-eyed, pleading, furious, still alive. Dark blood matted against his hair where the wound was. So Max strangled him.

He killed him twice and was sent to prison for seven years. When he got out Emma no longer loved him. In fact, she was horrified by what he had done. By then she had left the country.

———

They are at dinner when Elizabeth tells her this story— smoked pork, tortillas, beans, and they linger over espressos and mango pie. The thing is he didn't kill for love, says Elizabeth. Mainly he'd killed for money and it came out at the trial that he'd stolen twelve thousand dollars from Robert and planned to abscond with it the next day. A one-way ticket to New York.

Is it the fault of human beings that they are always so disappointing? Or is it the faulty universe? Paper lanterns swing from the branches of jacaranda in the outdoor patio and a young woman at the next table has taken the stage with her guitar. She has a remarkably clear voice and she sings the words of the song with terrific conviction, Caroline thinks, thinking also how rare it is to have such conviction. Even though she doesn't understand the words of the song, she feels she knows its meaning; that it speaks of hopefulness and perseverance in the face of impossible odds.

I like her voice, too, says Elizabeth, I like strength in a woman's voice because more than anything—more than love, more than money—it's what we need in our lives. Although I didn't always believe this.

———

I was 30 years old, already a widow, and so I left Mexico. I had loved two men. I couldn't imagine what would happen next in my life and then, slowly, I began to conceive of a life without love. When I lived in the woods, I began to heal people and I realized I had healed myself. Healing is simply that surplus of personal strength. It overflows your being.

One day I was in my garden—I grew herbs for healing and wildflowers for immense pleasure—and I was weeding and shaping the little rosemary bushes with my shears and I heard a man's voice. It was familiar to me in the way that a certain smell or shape from a dream is familiar. A recognition that was not absolute, but somehow resonant.

At first, I refused to look up; I concentrated on the sound of the voice and wondered if it could be, if it was possible. When I raised my head he was there, the man I had loved more than anyone, more than my husband. And I realized looking into his face that although I no longer loved him, I could love him again, and this terrified me.

We sat on my small porch until very late at night, drinking wine and talking about old times. Every once in a while, he would put out his hand to me, but I ignored it. I would refuse his hand in the air between us because to take it would have sealed my fate and I knew by then that I didn't want my fate sealed by him or anyone.

He wore a rumpled suit and his tie was askew on his neck. He had been looking for me for two years. His eyes had lines around them and when he spoke his lips trembled. Still, I refused him. After he left, I nursed my broken heart.

———

I don't understand, says Caroline. I don't understand how a person can live without passion. Tonight, on the way to the Instituto, I saw the strangest room. And she tells Elizabeth about the red room and the boy in the sepia photograph and the goose-necked lamp whose light looked like it would go on eternally. And her fantasy: that David had appeared with a new woman and that they were laughing together, joyous as he had never been with her.

That's the worst kind of fantasy, says Elizabeth. You do yourself in with that kind of fantasy, Caroline.

The singer is replacing her guitar in its case, collecting her things. She wears a silk jacket with little fish swimming up the sleeves; she slips a shiny hat over her shiny hair. How carefree she is in her youth! How her future expands before her! A young man with a red moustache kisses her on the cheek and she takes his arm.

I'm tired, says Elizabeth. She gives Caroline's hand a squeeze. And as she makes her way through the tables Caroline recalls what Max had said—that Elizabeth is a person who'd claimed her life. Unlike Caroline herself who is somewhat, what was it? Unfinished.

For example: she is tired, too, but disinclined to leave the restaurant patio with its drifting cigarette smoke, its whispered scraps of conversation. Nothing will happen, she is willing to bet, but she sits there anyway.

JAKE'S WIFE

THIS IS A STORY which begins in a strange country. It is the story of a woman existing in a certain historical time, in the history of the world and this country, which is not her own, and also within her own history, a history which is more than half-completed and so, she feels, is on the wane.

Perhaps it begins with the woman sitting in a central square, tree-filled and peopled, called El Jardin. She is sitting on a wrought iron bench which has been buried under so many layers of green paint that the details of the wrought iron, the petals on the acanthus, the intricacies of the scroll work, the hands, fingerprints, bits of tobacco, bird shit, conversations about weather, politics, love, the wind, breath, have been erased. Across from her, on an identical bench, a fat man in a leather jacket slumbers behind dark glasses. His head is back and over, angled in sleep, unbalanced at the neck; his hands barely clasp an orange folder which has slid to his knees.

Everywhere she looks are long rectangular posters announcing the election:

domingo

21 de Agosto

es

tu eleccion

diutados

senoradores

presidente

A mauve pigeon with orange feet wanders in a circle. An old man holds a stalk of balloons and a few toys—Mickey Mouses on bicycles, rubber lizards hung by their mouths whose striped tails jitter.

The day is overcast. The low-slung sky filled with bloated clouds. A truck rattles by with crates of soda bottles; someone claps; another shuffles; the pigeon lifts off, its wings clacking.

This is the scene in which the woman finds herself—or, to put it more actively, the scene in which she places herself, alone and observant.

She is trying to make sense of her life. Although she can't admit it, she is lonely. Whoever she is has escaped her. Let's leave it at that. Let's not belabor the point of her loneliness, of her escape from herself. Sometimes she sees it as shadows, the shadow slipping out from under the object, willful and inevitable, the shadow joining other shadows, who knows where they will go?

She is beset by a recurring fantasy that her life is about to end. She sees signs of it everywhere, in the little mint plant on the patio whose leaves have turned yellow and sparse, in the off-kilter chiming of the cathedral bells which mark a time unknown to anyone, as far as she can tell, and mostly in the way that people regard her, as if she were unremarkable.

And now the shuffler crosses her path, an old man wearing a straw hat, baggy black pants, and sport shoes that are too big, that make a sand-like sound like wire brushes on a drum. (Is he announcing something? A herald?) He shuffles with an orange bag slung over one arm, clutching a handful of pencils and at each large metal garbage pail he stops, rummaging. Is this a sign?

———

Let's hope not, says Martha. This is too depressing for me, I hope you're going to make it funnier. To be funny, I say, you've got to have perspective and it should be clear that this woman has no perspective. Well I hope she gets some fast, says Martha. And I hate that shuffler. Frankly, I think the shuffler is a mistake. You don't want a story about a search, this is your problem, I say to Martha. You want everything all fixed up and over with. That's not it, says Martha. Besides it's one thing for her to lack perspective; you yourself should have the intelligence to have perspective. You're the author. You have authorial intelligence; you should make the reader comfortable. Fiction should give us hope.

———

OK. A woman called Rose met a man called Jake. Once upon a time. She was thin with long hair (all her female characters have long hair), almost a child herself or, rather, though she was chronologically an adult, around 35, she continued to experience herself as if she were 19. Often she wondered where the years went. How fast they flew by her, or through her, like smoke. And since her past was in fact hazy, because she had a poor memory, she often felt the past was a series of dreams; they had color and vague shapes she couldn't quite visualize. There had been a marriage and births and a divorce. There had been an education, a coming-out party, countless trysts in the moonlight, among them a hayride with a boy called Arthur. There had been swimming lessons, piano lessons, French lessons, painting lessons, and a few despised tennis lessons.

She was a painter and since she painted what was there, right in front of her eyes—a still life with a fan and a pitcher, a naked model with a bikini line—the past was unimportant.

She met Jake at an opening for a sculptor whose name and work she quickly forgot. She had been standing by a punch bowl eating chips. Her mood had been low. She gazed at the clump of people who mingled with such ease before her and envied them their benevolent spirits and laughter. A woman wearing an enormous turquoise ring was talking about pottery. With her hands, she made the shape of an urn in the air and then went on to describe the glazes, which were not only distinctive in color but hard to come by. I got them in Mexico, the woman explained. Oh, but I've always wanted to go to Mexico, said one of her companions, a man in a tan suit. You should, you should! said the woman. Mexico is the nuts! Take me with you, said the man, next time you go. I will! said the woman. I'm going tomorrow!

Then Rose sidled to the other end of the punch bowl table where she met Jake. Jake was a young man who wore a diamond earring and tight leather pants. He was tearing at a hangnail with his teeth.

Are you superstitious? he asked Rose. No, she said. Why? Just wondering, he said. He looked her up and down and, truth be told, Rose looked terrific that night. She wore a black linen dress and a string of pearls. Her hair, parted in the middle, hung in silky flaps on either side of her face. She had on olive green eyeshadow. You're cute, said Jake. Did you say your name was Barbara? Hardly, said Rose. Suzanne? No, said Rose. Neither of those names remotely resembled mine.

This is how it started. He took her home in a 20-year-old VW bug with loose ball joints. For this reason, the steering was not what it might have been. More than once Rose screamed, Have you completely lost your mind? because she was terrified. She also screamed: I'm a mother, be careful of my life! At home she had two children who counted on her for love and food.

Finally, after an excruciating hour, they pulled into her driveway. Thank

God, she said, clutching her purse to her ribcage. What time is it anyway? asked Jake. It's two, said Rose, the babysitter will be having a fit. How do you get out of this car anyway? Two pm? said Jake. I'd better zip out, I've got surgery in the morning. Surgery? said Rose. What are they going to operate on? Your eyesight? Actually, said Jake, I'm doing the operation. Nose job. You're a doctor? said Rose. Wonders never cease. Why are you so dumbfounded? I would have thought you'd have a better car for one thing, which, by the way, I seem to be trapped in. Oh that, said Jake. Busted door handle. I'll go around.

And so Jake opened the door for Rose and shook her hand firmly and told her he'd call within the week. They were, at this point, standing under the maple tree that grew on the edge of the driveway and the leaves were brushing their heads. Jake tore off one of the green pods, split it, and pasted it on his nose. Didn't you used to do this as a kid? he asked. I don't remember, said Rose. Even with the thing on his nose, he was handsome. He had brown eyes with little flecks of yellow. His teeth were charmingly crooked as was his nose.

Jake didn't call that week and therefore she forgot about him. Plus, she had other boyfriends. Presently she was having an affair with a man called Mark who, although a junkie, was a marvelous cook. The kids loved him. But it depressed her to think she'd spend the rest of her life with a dope fiend. He used to shoot up in the bathroom and she was always having to shield this activity from her innocent and adorable children.

Also, he was too thin. He felt like a little lost child in her arms, a starving Biafran or a third world beggar. But perhaps this is why she stuck by him.

The next time she saw Jake was at O'Hare airport in Chicago. She was between flights, on her way to see her sister in Salt Lake City and Jake was on his way to LA to deliver a paper entitled "Loose Skin: Necks, Jowls, and their Vicissitudes." Don't you think the title is a little flip? she asked. For a surgical conference? What do you know about surgical conferences? he asked. He wore torn dungarees, a plaid shirt and a tie. He had replaced the diamond in his ear with a dangling map of Texas. Over one arm he carried a tweed sports jacket. His loafers, she noticed, had dimes in them.

Over cocktails in the murky light of the lounge he took her hand. I've been thinking about you constantly, he said. I find that hard to believe, she said. Why? Because I didn't call? he said. Frankly, yes, said Rose. Well, I tried, I can't tell you how many times I let the phone ring and then hung up when you answered. It was just too scary. You're incredibly childish, said Rose, although she allowed a glimmer of a smile to cross her lips. She covered it up by sipping a cocktail, a loathsome orange concoction with a stemless maraschino cherry floating on the top. Besides, she added, that was months ago. I'm sure you have other things on your mind at this point. Not at all, he said and he whipped a folded napkin out of his jeans pocket and read aloud to her the following:

> To Rose
> With her hair and nose
> You'd think she was a Rose
> Though she's a little chilly
> Like a lily. etc.

When did you write that? she asked. On the plane, he said. Amazing, she said, and she left her hand in his because she'd forgotten to remove it and now it was too late.

Rose didn't go to Salt Lake City (she called her sister from the hotel) and Jake likewise blew off the conference. Together they took sheets of "Loose Skin: Jowls, Necks and their Vicissitudes" and made them into little paper airplanes and sailed them around the hotel room after sex. They spent a week in Chicago, mostly in that room.

Rose was in love. I'm in love with you, Jake, only it terrifies me. I'm not used to a feeling of this magnitude. Don't worry about it, said Jake, I'm not either. He was brushing her hair. If I hadn't been a surgeon I would have been a hairdresser. I love this. My wife never lets me touch her hair, it gives her the creeps. Your wife? said Rose. Why didn't you tell me this before? I was waiting for the opportune time, said Jake. God, said Rose. This puts a whole new perspective on things. I suppose, said Jake. I was thinking you could be my mistress. I don't think I'm into being anyone's mistress, said Rose. They say in that direction lies pain and heartache. Also, you are a creep. You should have told me about your wife beforehand. What's she like anyway?

She's very clean, said Jake. She loves eggs. She hates baseball. She has a cat named Willie. Here he paused and looked at his knees. That's it? said Rose. That's about all I know about her. She's not forthcoming. This is weird, said Rose.

But she became Jake's mistress anyway. It wasn't too bad in the beginning. She kicked out Mark, the junkie, and the kids had no trouble adjusting to Jake, who was much more cheerful and energetic than Mark had been. Why don't you divorce Sara? Rose said one night. They were making pesto in the blender. Jake tossed in a handful of pignoles and said he didn't want to. It's too much of a hassle, he said. I hate hassles. She thinks I've been faithful. So what? said Rose. It's time she woke up. Jake put the blender on high and closed his eyes. The thing is, he said over the noise of the blender, I still love her. What? said Rose. How could you love her? You said you hardly know her? That's true and that's why I love her, I think. She's so inaccessible. She keeps my desire alive. Sometimes she sits on the roof with the cat just staring into space and, like the cat, her eyes eventually begin to close. It's very endearing. She's very small and shiny, a small shiny thing is what I call her. It's true that she hates to talk but she shows her devotion to me in other ways. What about me? says Rose. How do I fit into all this? Her lower lip was trembling. You're my mistress, said Jake. It's a different type of thing. He sat down heavily on one of the white kitchen chairs. I don't know how you fit in, to be honest. But perhaps that's the way it is with mistresses. You probably never should have involved yourself with me.

———

That's it? says Martha. I don't think you should just leave her there. Poised between the pesto and Jake in that kitchen, a look of horror on her face. Maybe not, I say, but that's the way I see it. I see him confessing his love for his wife and then the story's over. She breaks up with him, is depressed for a while, gets over it, meets someone else, blah blah blah. Thank God she meets someone else, says Martha. I hope this new person will be worthy of her. What makes you think she's worthy of anyone? I say.

———

In this part of the city, fireworks soar like angels and she is reading a book about the unevenness of history, situated as she is in it, looming on either side of her, greater than she. Enormous walls of history like the looms in Martha's studio, streams of colors being spun as she reads, in the moment of, without looking back. History doesn't look back, she makes a note of this so that she can continue without that "irritating grasping after" that Keats spoke about. Anything to get perspective: the long lines of the buildings changing colors, shaping themselves rectangular, and old stones of amber and earth and gray. Whatever crosses and recrosses has, she realizes, the possibility of hope.

———

Eventually she meets someone else. A painter. A mortician. A stockbroker. Her life could be catalogued by such romantic episodes. Her life is both happy and unhappy, like anyone's. Finally, she has gotten to the point where she no longer obsesses about the future. She sits on the green bench in El Jardin and watches the man who sells those spongey toys that wiggle on the pavement and amuse the children. She says: We are alike, that man and I, and her eyes fill and her heart chakra breaks open and she accepts the world exactly as it is.

I don't believe you, says Martha.

JULIAN'S BIRDS

DR. F. IS A stout, freckled man with delicate hands who, for a living, adjusts chakras and mends auras. He is a healer, a curandero of sorts. He pays 900 pesos a month for the use of a room in the back of Julian's house and in this room, he sees his clients. The room overlooks a garden of banana trees and oleander and a dirty white wall belonging to the neighbor and a gigantic tree in which birds harbor and wail into the night, sometimes until 2 am. They make sounds as if they are rapping on Dr. F.'s window or clinking teacups together or barking like puppies or, worst of all, groaning in unbearable, strangulated unhappiness, like human beings in a mental ward. The birds' noises drive everybody, not only Dr. F., crazy, and so Julian has recently decided to have the tree removed. The trouble is that you can't fell a tree without special permission from the Presidente and so the best that can be done is to hire a man to come and lop off the leafy branches where the nests are. In this way, it is hoped, the birds will leave, and Dr. F.'s clients will enjoy a more serene treatment. And who knows, it might even remedy the mosquito problem—those mosquitos who, because Dr. F. forgets sometimes to close his sliding screen door, drone around the patients' heads and bite them on the arms and ankles during the actual time of treatment when they are supposed to be lying still.

This is what Dr. F. does: He positions the patient on the bed and tells them to close their eyes. Then he goes into the bathroom and washes up. Then he comes out and, standing over the patient, takes in a deep breath of air and says a prayer to the cosmos. Then he places his small hands on various parts of the patient's body, beginning with the head and working his way down. His hands become very hot during this procedure and the patient can smell the warm smell of sweet, inexpensive soap on Dr. F.'s hands and the heat and soap smell permeate the patient's body until everything is in balance. Afterwards, Dr. F. asks the patient how she feels and the patient, who doesn't speak Spanish very well, says Bien, gracias, and then she and Dr. F. share a companionable cigarette and remark on the birds and on the mosquitos.

The patient has been feeling off-balance lately and so it is fortuitous really that Dr. F. has come into her life. She is suffering from heartbreak. She fell in love with someone and then that person went off and married someone else and moved to Paraguay with his new wife. She had been in the habit of loving this person, of having this person in her life, and now she is left with an emptiness in her heart, a round blank cold space—she can feel its marbled contours against her ribcage—that used to be filled with love. She walks around in a daze, therefore, and has no taste for anything in the world. Mainly she wants to sleep, hoping that, at the end of a long nap, she will wake up and have returned to normal. But this hasn't happened.

Dr. F. says she must have patience, that melancholy and nostalgia are not so easily banished. That she should eat some of Lupe's good enchiladas and some rice with corn. Maybe a little chicken in white sauce or even a mango. She should nourish herself. He gives her a tea to drink three times a day, but the tea gives her gas. She is happiest lying on Dr. F.'s bed, on the nylon bedspread with the orange ruffle, having the mosquitos whine in her ears and bite her feet. Here she can at least steel herself against their assaults and lie perfectly still. Each permutation in the atmosphere registers the volatility of her psyche, she feels: the warm, over-fragrant hands of Dr. F.—a sensation both pleasant and unpleasant—the mosquitos, and, of course, the maddening racket of the birds who she, like everyone else, would like to murder.

———

At 6 am, when the man and his assistant arrive to trim the tree, Julian is still asleep. He is dreaming he is on a ship with his dog and that the ship's railings are pure gold and that the remarkably handsome captain has kissed him on the mouth. But when he looks into the sky of this dream, the moon is covered with ants. The beautiful looking captain then screams in horror and covers his mouth, like Ingrid Bergman in *Gaslight*. This is when Julian awakens to the sounds of a chainsaw outside his window and he remembers that today is the day, the last day of the birds, thank God.

The man is charging 600 pesos for the tree trimming, but it's worth every fucking cent, says Julian to his housemate Carla. Will the birds die? says Carla. She wants them out of her life but is not sure she can contend with the guilt. Ambivalence is her permanent state of mind. Let's hope so, says Julian. Let's hope they die painful deaths and burn in hell.

Carla remembers a friend from a few years ago who said that to a man who dumped her for another woman. I hope you burn in hell, the friend had said, and Carla had both been horrified and impressed at such a bald statement of rage. She herself had not the courage to say such a thing to the person she'd loved; in fact, she said nothing when he told her of his plans to marry this woman and she said nothing when he packed his things into a plastic lawn-and-leaf bag and moved out of her room. Nor did she say anything when she passed him in El Jardin, his arm encircling the broad shoulders of his esposa-to-be, who had black eyes and perfect teeth and smiled at Carla insincerely.

Those pinche men are going to kill themselves, says Julian, looking out the window at one in a high branch with the chainsaw, making wild passes at a flock of leaves that are entangled in a very pretty orange fungus.

Then he tells Carla his dream. Ants on the moon, says Carla. I kind of like that. It was horrifying, says Julian. Did you kiss with tongues? asks Carla. Unfortunately not, darling, says Julian. He adjusts the sash of his Chinese robe. Although does this ever happen to you? Do you ever dream about someone totally unfamiliar and then meet them in real life? I have a feeling I'm going to meet this guy. Don't laugh at me, I'm very psychic.

At this moment a big piece of tree falls on Julian's favorite banana tree and he lets out a shriek. I don't believe these assholes! he says, and he rushes into the garden.

By afternoon, the tree men have completed their work. They have killed six banana trees, smashed a stone garden ornament in the form of a squirrel and put a hole in Dr. F.'s screen door. Aside from the mangled leafed branches—these scattered across the garden's breadth, still choked in fungus whose little orange globes jitter in the wind—and the nests, perfectly intact, finely crafted, brown and abandoned, there are birds everywhere, in death throes: some twitching under the oleander and others limping around the swimming pool in a lugubrious parade.

I hate this, says Julian. Will you just look at them? Because no one, not Dr. F. or Carla or Lupe, had ever actually seen the birds up close before. Once in a while, a large flapping wing high in the branches, against a cloud or rocketing over the dirty white wall in search of fish from the park's ponds, but never this intimately, and it fills them all with dread. The birds are immense and speckled and vulturish with hooded heads sunken into their necks. But their most dreadful aspect are their long green legs and

feet, which trod solemnly, vengefully upon the white plaster. Whatever
the species—no one seems to be able to identify it—there is something
monstrous and brutal about them. One is twitching outside the door
near the dog's bowl and Julian throws a red towel over it. Rest in peace,
fucker, he says.

Do you think we could shoot them? he asks Carla seriously, later. They
are drinking glasses of jamaica on the patio and smoking cigarettes. Dr.
F. laughs. Bad karma, he says.

———

Eight months ago Carla met Miguel in the park. She had been jogging.
He had been reading a newspaper. She had noticed him the third time
around, faded blue-jeaned legs stretched in front of him and crossed at the
ankles, dark glasses, a kind of tender insouciance about the mouth. Also his
fingers, which held the edges of the paper in a particularly unmindful way,
so that its pages fluttered in his hands and slipped over his knees.

On her fourth round she noticed his shoes—old leather hiking boots with
mended, mismatched laces—and by her fifth, he had tucked the paper into
a plastic bolsa and was simply staring at a crop of pink iris, which is when
she noticed his hair, which sloped into one eye and glided down the nape of
his neck, barely riddling the collar of his lumpy wool sweater. In retrospect,
there had been something managed about his negligence, an artfulness that
should have alerted her to the dangers and deviations within. Instead, she
was impressed by his subtlety, his charming self-design. And so on her sixth
round, winded and aching, sweat agreeably trickling down her cheeks and
beneath her arms and the little caves of her breasts, she'd approached him.

Please be seated, he'd said. He refused to smile. Your eyes, he told her,
are the color of Madonna's, green and black. Mater Dolorosa. What do
you do, in your life?

You mean to survive? she said. It was a question that dismayed her.

You don't seem like a tourist, he said, you're not happy enough. His English was almost impeccable; he'd studied in Chicago for five years.

Actually, she said, I make hats. Hats? he said. Is it profitable? Not terribly, she said. He appealed to her enormously. Pero lo quiero mucho. He laughed. Her Spanish, as aforementioned, was imperfect. The best way to learn Spanish is to take a Mexican lover, he told her. He flashed her a brilliant smile. He had beautiful teeth and she thought to tell him, but she decided against it.

What was beautiful about them? asks Julian.

They were perfectly imperfect, says Carla. Gapped in the front and a bit crooked, but lovely nonetheless. You know those people who are negligent and exquisite at the same time? Negligent because exquisite and probably vice versa?

I think you're well rid of him, says Julian who is furiously chopping cloves of garlic for a bean dip.

One of the many things Carla admires about Julian is his way of chopping things. For example, the garlic forms a neat, symmetrical mound that is entirely aesthetically pleasing. Then he sweeps it into a bowl with the garbanzos. I think you're well rid of him, repeats Julian. He was very dirty. I'll bet he never changed his underwear.

He had a great sense of humor, Carla tells Julian.

Apparently, says Julian, and he looks at her with significance.

But I think I was happy with him, although to be honest my memory of him is growing dim.

Out of sight, out of mind, says Julian, mashing the garbanzos. He does it with a stone pestle, traditionally, then he lets her lick off the remains, as if she were a child. Don't dribble that on you, he says. By his own admission, he is anal-retentive, fretful, afraid of disease.

Carla closes her eyes. She herself is not so fastidious—either in life or appearance. At this moment, for example, there are lines of dirt under her fingernails and her hair is uncombed. She has bags under her eyes (from weeping) and she chain-smokes, letting the ashes fall where they may. She is not getting any younger. Her air of tragedy, she agrees with Julian, is incredibly boring.

Who cares if Miguel, the love of her life, is lost to her, making his way through the wilds of Paraguay with his new wife? They are tourists, they are gazing up at buildings, they are standing in queues waiting for tickets for this or that attraction. He has left her with only a few images and these, she has to admit, though they are persistent, have a depleted, lifeless quality: His sleeping face on the pillow, the violet shadow of his beard, his agile fingers with their bitten nails. When the stars come out, he once said, we are up there, we were always up there. But he'd also added, circumspectly, we are in two different worlds in this lifetime. Perhaps in the next we will have our chance. Such grandiose romance is her special vulnerability.

Although when I think about it, when I turn my coldest mind to it, I am not sure what I loved about him.

There you go, said Julian. That's because there was nothing to love. Julian is a pragmatist about all lives except his own, which is a wreck. Like her, he has had a series of disastrous love affairs. Plus he has cancer and that has given him a certain toughness.

Today I saw my dream captain, he tells Carla. Are you amazed?

No way! says Carla. Was he as beautiful in real life?

Even more so, says Julian, but he was with his wife. He never even looked at me. I think he's a banker.

How disappointing, Carla says, but it's always the way with dreams I think.

Isn't it though? says Julian.

This bean dip is fab, says Carla.

I know, says Julian, but I wish you wouldn't call it bean dip.

———

The room Dr. F. rents from Julian consists of a bed (double), a built-in settee with gold upholstered foam pads and six little cushions of a varied print against the wall, a '20s fainting couch covered in beige velvet (Dr. F. imported this from his home in Querétero), two gold vinyl chairs and a rug. The rug is one of those frequently used in bathrooms, to cover the commode. It is pink plush with blue and yellow flecks and contrasts vulgarly with the décor in the rest of the room, its scrubbed pale walls (sponge-painted by Julian) and the long drapes, cream-colored and green. Also, Dr. F. has replaced the bedspread provided with the room with one of his own—an orange nylon with a ruffle. This all to Julian's dismay. Can you imagine? says Julian to his friends, taking them through the room on Dr. F.'s off-days. Who would do this? he says. And then he shows them the bathroom, where installed on the toilet seat and on the commode, are flecked, plush covers which match the rug.

Julian has had two bouts with cancer which gives him the right to be unkind. Also, he has impeccable taste. People from all over the world consult him on their interiors. Whether to hang the Rivera lithograph above the bed or over the settee in the alcove. Whether to gold leaf the armoire. Julian himself owns two wing-backed chairs that used to belong to Joan Crawford and a collection of ancient Chinese pottery.

When his beautiful blond hair fell out in chunks during chemo, he wore a velvet turban with an old cameo affixed to the front. He looked like a tall, elegant woman.

Carla keeps her room simple, the better to hold her ample tragedy. The better to scatter her belongings, her books, her half-filled bottles of cosmetics and wine. Her hairbrushes. Her mail.

Dear Carla, Miguel writes on the back of a postcard of a pointed Paraguayan mountain. She kicks it out of her path.

———

In between clients, Dr. F. smokes and gazes out of the window at the birds who are in recovery, now roosting on what is left of the tree, that is to say on the enormous bare branches that the tree men have refused to sever. It is most unsightly, but its starkness brings Dr. F. a certain peace. At least now he can see the birds. He can count them: 11. They still make noise, unfortunately, and so the tree venture has not been a success.

Dr. F. sighs. The tree venture has not been a success and Julian's blood pressure is rising again, which is not good for his cancer. Already, there are little holes appearing in his aura.

Dr. F. loves Julian, not in a romantic way, but in the high spiritual way that is Dr. F.'s gift to the world. His love, he believes, makes possible his healing. Sometimes he feels it swelling against his ribcage and then he knows his powers are at their full swing. Other times, such as when his wife De De, the tarot reader, shouts at him for being forgetful, he feels this love ebb and shrivel and he has to focus inward on his own chakras and find the blockages.

Now he is waiting for the client who doesn't speak Spanish . This is always a difficulty. He has to remember to speak very slowly and when she responds he is not at all sure that she has understood his instructions.

This tea gives me gas, she tells him today. I will give you another tea to counteract the gas, he tells her. What if I stop taking this tea? she asks. Wouldn't that be a more efficient way of counteracting the gas? Dr. F. offers her a cigarette and lights one himself. He looks into the garden where one of the birds is rooting under a bush. Look, he says finally, if you stop taking the tea your colon will become inflamed and you will feel sad. You must learn to live in the here and now, he tells her. This is a phrase she doesn't understand. Either in English or Spanish, he thinks. Here is your life, he says, pointing to the garden, the bare tree, the sky with its one cloud, the pink oleander. Here it is, he says. She looks baffled.

———

Compared to Julian, Carla's life is not so bad. Julian lives with the fact of his own mortality every day, whereas Carla, neurotic but relatively healthy, has only heartbreak to contend with. Julian tells her this, not in a mean-spirited way but in order to snap her out of it. Miguel has written her a postcard from Paraguay. He is bored. He broke his arm in a freak accident. He is unhappy with his new wife. She purchased a six-pack of jockey shorts which she insists he wear. How incredible! says Carla, him telling me this. Good for her, says Julian approvingly. Obviously, he's with the right woman.

How can you say that? How can you be so glib? Carla is crying into a paper napkin. He is such a child, she says. Together we were children. He used to tell me I was beautiful.

Which was a lie, says Julian. You're quite attractive, but I wouldn't say beautiful. I am beautiful.

This is true; he used to be the Givenchy house model and wore only a pair of underpants and a long Oxford shirt. Now he is too pale and his posture is a bit stooped, but his eyes are a startling blue and his face is long and aristocratic, fine-boned.

She is, at best, sexy. She has a good figure. Once a man told her her body was a poem but her face was a bit haggard. She hated that word, haggard. It made her think of hags and aging, of her mother, now in her eighties, traversing the back yard with a cane, swiping at the dead tulip heads because she no longer has the ability to stoop and pick them off.

All week, they've been preparing food for a party to be held on Saturday night. Carla lights another cigarette.

Maybe he really needs me.

Excuse me while I vomit into this salsa, says Julian.

It wouldn't make any difference, says Carla meanly. It already tastes like shit.

———

Everybody has tragedy in their lives. What is bearable is bearable. What is not is denied. Think of the birds high in the empty tree limbs, roosting there unhappily. Or of Julian whose plan to banish them has misfired. Or of Miguel, his arm in a sling in Paraguay because he fell from a bar stool. Or of Carla weeping, weeping over what she can never have.

Even Dr. F., seemingly so calm, has had his share of bad luck. His wife, De De, has grown skinny and sallow-skinned. She nags him. She has visions which bode ill for his career.

But without tragedy, how would it be possible to experience the good parts of life? This argument is simplistic, but undeniable.

Carla lies awake listening to the birds' hopeless cries and is no longer irritated by them. Now her response is closer to regret. The birds, it was finally discovered, are baby egrets, speckled and ugly like the duckling of fairy tale fame. Soon they would be white, majestic; their mawkishness would change to grace. If only she were still young, she thinks. If only she had a future.

Julian, hearing the birds, turns up the volume on his remote. He is watching a movie starring Fred Astaire and Cyd Charisse. Cyd is playing the part of a Russian communist who is being corrupted by capitalism and Fred. She's a very bad actress.

Dr. F. tosses and turns beneath the orange nylon bedspread. The mosquitos are getting to him.

Carla is remembering a particular conversation with Miguel, one in which he told her that they were exactly alike. Too much so, he'd said. We're both wanderers. We need a steadying hand.

However, Cyd has terrific legs, the best in the biz. She is dangling a pair of American nylons from behind a white screen. She reaches in a drawer and produces a forbidden negligee. She dances.

Whereas Miguel, pobrecito, is laboring over his new wife who is wearing a green sweat suit. She closes her eyes and is craving a sandwich, chicken and avocado on one of those fresh bolillos. In Paraguay, such things are not to be had.

The really terrible thing about life, reflects Carla, is that it is always the same. It always seems to circle back to the same spot, it travels in a groove, and the high points are the same along the way—scenic overlooks or gas stations with concession stands. This is what you realize when you're old (Carla is 45), but when you're young—she pauses in her thoughts for a moment to listen to the baby egrets' screech in a particularly long series—you think everything will change, accumulate and thus change. But nothing accumulates, only repetition: the sky with its wallowing clouds and the enormous green of the elegant leaves after a rain; bougainvillea spilling over the neighbor's rock walls and the color of the stones, orange and violet, like bruises.

Dr. F. is trying to sleep, but the bed provided by Julian is too hard. It digs into his rib cage. Then there is the problem of where to put the arm; the pillow is like a rock. The Mayans used stones as pillows; difficult to imagine this. He is glad, nonetheless, that De De is not here to give her long impatient groans. On his days at Julian's she generally stays in Querétero. He goes back and forth, a commuter. He is trying to do good in the world but there is so much resistance. If only people would eat correctly; if only they would be kinder to one another. If only the damn birds would go to sleep.

Julian is falling asleep. The remote glides from his hand and clatters to the floor. Cyd Charisse and Fred Astaire are kissing, but Julian has missed this important moment. Their lips touch; they dance; they will live happily ever after.

————

If Carla had come to this place earlier in her life, who knows what might have happened? She might have married someone like Miguel and raised a flock of tiny dark-haired children with serious eyes. She might have become the mistress of a wealthy industrialist and been ensconced in a graceful Spanish colonial with a courtyard and lace curtains.

Instead, she makes hats, collecting fabrics from the second-hand tables at Tuesday market—velvets, silk paisleys, scraps of worsted wool, felts, printed damasks, taffetas, linens—and concocts them. Flat disks layered with veils as wispy as breezes; deep, nubby chenilles with bands of tiny leaded soldiers marching across the brims; hats with birds' nests or fabricated ant colonies, golf balls, nasturtium leaves; hats that tell jokes or celebrate occasions or mourn for dead uncles; lively and informative hats; tragic, weeping, hysterical hats adorned with aigrettes and buttons and faux vegetables; utterly banal hats shaped like cones. The hats, she likes to think, are her statement about the world and its pathetic, elegant triviality.

She works in a studio with a shop front window facing the street, and in the window, she displays the hats on black mannequin heads—today an exotic felt Panama and a little pagoda hat. She herself faces away from the window to work on her machine because it is better for business to allow the customer to imagine that the hats spring from a source nobler than the toils of a middle-aged woman with bags under her eyes.

If you didn't smoke those bags would disappear, says Julian. You'd look ten years younger. Well, five.

When Julian visits he is dismayed at her lack of organization. How about if we gather all the beige bits into one basket, then you will at least know where to look. Looking is part of my process, she says. It sparks my creativity. Also I rather like the clutter of this place; it's artsy, I think.

Julian rolls his eyes. Artsy fartsy, he says, I hate that look. Reminds me of dirty hippies with venereal diseases.

Of which I was one.

Of which you are no longer, thank you God. Thank the lord you're past your prime hippy-ness. Darling, he adds as an afterthought.

Today he has brought her a beautiful piece of damask, purple and gold, and some linen he dyed with tea. Do you adore this or not? he asks. Is it fabulous or not?

When a man arrives at the door with a cluster of wooden toy violins spray painted in yellow, Julian says, Do I look like I want a toy violin? Do I? For your niete? says the man. Do I look like a grandfather? Do I? Julian can always make Carla laugh. Even the man with the violins laughs good-naturedly.

Anyway, I saw him again today, says Julian.

Don't tell me, says Carla. She is hand stitching an aigrette plume onto a piece of red velvet and she is thinking that her eyesight is getting worse. Your banker.

Today he was selling those rubber lizards in El Jardin. There was no wife.

Did he see you? asks Carla. Did he wink or anything?

Life is so tragic, says Julian, especially for the tragedy-prone. He looked right through me.

Outside a procession of little girls goes by. The tallest carries a large plaque of the Virgin of Guadalupe. They walk solemnly, but out of step. They are the most beautiful thing Carla has seen all day. She will make a hat to commemorate them.

———

On Saturday, party preparations accelerate. Julian has made lentil balls and bean dip, mango chutney from scratch, salmon mousse and liver pate. Carla has made pesto to stuff into tiny red potatoes; Lupe is cutting up the crudités and has a fresh pot of salsa on the stove. Also, there will be mushrooms in the chile, fresh camarones, chicken legs in garlic and lemon sauce, and cake. Dr. F. will bring the cake from Querétero, though it makes Carla nervous to think about it. Supposing it has no sugar, she tells Julian. Don't be ridiculous, says Julian. He smokes.

The party is for Gabriel, his 40th birthday, and the irony is that Julian is having an off-season with Gabriel. Gabriel has been pissing him off deliberately, according to Julian, but Carla says it's just Gabriel's way.

He's a painter and gets sullen; he doesn't always appear grateful; he refuses to understand Anglo mentality, even if some of them are his best friends. Now he wants the party to start at a different hour and he wants there to be only rum. No one wants anything but rum. It's the best drink, says Gabriel. Also he wants a few more guests to be included, people he forgot to put on the guest list, but now he has reconsidered. You're an ass-fucking-hole, says Julian, but he says this after he hangs up the phone with Gabriel.

Carla thinks about Miguel as she stuffs teaspoonfuls of pesto into the cavities of potatoes. She prods her memory of him, like a tongue on a sore tooth, calling forth the pain. Soon her stomach is in knots. Miguel dancing with her in the salsa bar, closer and closer until their hips move in a fine groove with each other; Miguel pouring her a glass of milk, Drink up, he'd said, you need to be healthy; Miguel laughing; Miguel crying when he told her about his new woman, his marriage. It's not that I want to. It's my culture. I feel forced. Well then, Carla had said. She almost managed an insincere shrug. It has become her philosophy not to interfere with people's decisions.

Julian is slicing the mushrooms so perfectly Carla stops just to watch. He doesn't look up; he is thinking that despite what everybody tells him about himself, he cannot feel beautiful or accomplished. Despite six years of heavy-duty therapy in LA and despite an entourage of glamorous lovers, both male and female, and despite the treatments of Dr. F., whose effects don't seem to last more than a few hours. Now there is a pain in his shoulder he has been trying to ignore for days.

And the birds have begun their twilight ritual. *Tut tu tu, raaaa, sqauuuuu, yuh.* And Lupe is thinking it's getting late, she has to check on her children and dress for the party. She will wear a red dress which her grandmother embroidered around the hem with little stars.

And Carla will wear suspender pants and a silver lamé shirt and Julian will wear all black, jeans, jacket, shirt (linen) and Dr. F. will wear what he always wears, a checked shirt whose buttons pop over his belly and khaki pants, whereas De De will dress in a fancy gold dress with a bustle and white stiletto heels, a plunging neckline to show off what's left of her thin bust.

And whether Gabriel will wear his little leather jacket that the maid shrunk by washing in water with detergent or whether he will wear his fleece-lined vest, he is not certain. He will not wear the hat he has been wearing to shield his bald spot from the sun, even though he's been wearing it to the bars lately.

———

The birds are strangely silent. They sit on the bare limbs of the tree and stare at Carla who is watching them from her window. Behind, the sky is flecked with little purple dots and for once the Parroquia bells can be heard and the children playing basketball in the park and a trumpet belonging to a parade somewhere. It is all very beautiful, but she is not so sure that truth is beauty and beauty is truth and that that is all she has to know. It seems to her that life gets geometrically more depressing the longer one lives it. One of the more depressing facts is that in love one is always an adolescent.

Here's the truth: Miguel used Carla shamefully. He moved into her room, slept in her bed, took up her closet and drawer space so that she had to move her sweaters to an inaccessible cupboard too high for her to reach, ate the food she purchased for Julian's fridge, fucked her when he felt like it (this goes without saying), removed her old Kilim rug from the floor (didn't like the colors), destroyed at least one hat-in-progress the night he came home drunk and vomiting (he said he thought the lump of fabrics on the floor was the dog, though why he would vomit on the dog is still a mystery), borrowed money, stole money from her wallet, ripped her orange poetry festival tee shirt, misplaced her books, and was unfaithful. And lied about it. The unbeautiful truth. Now she lives with a homosexual who has cancer; visits, twice a week, a quack who gives her odd-tasting teas which make her fart; makes hats whose drama and elegance are lost on everyone except her. And makes no money.

She lights a cigarette and blows smoke into the window glass where it billows back in a large, gray, toxic cloud. One by one, the birds come out of their reveries and begin to scream.

———

Julian is shaving, but it hurts his shoulder to do so. He has become accustomed to ignoring the irreparable in his body and focusing on the redeemable—his blue eyes, his teeth, and his new hair which he blows dry so that it hangs straight and blond to his shoulders. Like silk, Carla told him once. But what good does it do to him? Lately, he has been seeing his dream captain everywhere and always in different guises. Today, three times—a bartender who politely served him a gin and tonic, a candy salesman driving a white van who braked for Julian to cross Canal, and a woman carrying a baby in a striped roboso. He must be going mad.

———

No one knows how the typhoid began. It is sweeping the city now and it is inconvenient, if not irritating, not to have a food handler like Typhoid Mary to blame for it. The symptoms are another thing people are uncertain about. A terrible pain in the stomach; perhaps diarrhea, perhaps headache and fatigue. But the symptoms mimic those of hundreds of other ailments we are familiar with: amoebic dysentery, cholera, even

turista. If you were to stand in El Jardin in the middle of the day you'd
see everyone racing to the lab with stool samples in little cups. Where
did you eat last night? What are your symptoms? How many times did
you shit? Que color?

Tonight we are going to Julian's party and so there's no need to worry.
Most of us are on the mend anyway. Dr. F. and his wife De De have been
immune, so far, to the illness, since they live in Querétero and since they
wouldn't dream of buying burritos from the street. De De, nonetheless,
feels achy. She says she feels a vision coming on. A big one, she says. She
gauges its importance by the intensity of her discomfort before. And
today, she tells Dr. F., my limbs are in knots. If I didn't know better I'd
say I had typhoid.

Dr. F. sighs sorrowfully. He had been looking forward to Julian's party
and now he has a feeling he will not be able to go. De De is lying on
their double bed with the drapes drawn and she is gazing steadfastly at
the statue of the Virgin of Guadalupe which is placed in the center of
the altar she constructed for Quetzalcoatl. Oh Virgin, my mother! she
cries. A wand of light passes through the chink between the drapes and
it falls precisely on the Virgin's face. Is this an accident? Then there is
a purple egg in front of De De's eyes and little spots of gray and some
pink color shooting across. She feels as though she is too heavy for the
bed, too heavy for this world, her legs like lead weights and her head as
if cemented to the pillow.

Oh Virgin, mia, grant me strength, she whispers into the room, where
at the moment Dr. F. is rummaging in a drawer for a pair of socks.

Then two smoky wings fly across the room (one following the other
and flapping in synchronicity, like dancers) and attach themselves to each
of the shoulders of De De. Dr. F. stops his sock searching just to watch
this complex operation and to watch the wings themselves, which are as
big as doors and seemingly constructed of feathers.

Then she is flying around the room in her nightgown, his wife, and she is saying, Fernando, I feel much better, if you could hand up my stockings while you're at it in that drawer, I'd appreciate it.

And Gabriel, who also doesn't have typhoid, is at any rate in no mood for a party. For one thing, he'd forgotten about it and made other plans, but just now someone called to remind him that the party is in his honor and that he had to go. Maybe I could just go for a little while, he said, but his friend said, No you absolutely have to go to the whole party, not just part of it. So now he is faced with the task of finding this beautiful woman who he thinks he is really falling in love with and breaking their date. He could bring her along to the party, of course, but she is so beautiful that other men will be crowding around her all night and this will annoy him. It's a dilemma and it gives him a pain in his stomach that is suspiciously like typhoid, but isn't, he knows.

And the beautiful woman is at this moment at the lab with her stool sample surrounded by lab technicians and a few passersby who have seen her through the window and couldn't resist entering the lab and standing next to her and listening with interest to what the technicians are saying which is that she doesn't have either typhoid or amoebas, but that maybe she should take some pills anyway, just to be on the safe side and come back in the morning.

And Carla is putting the finishing touches on a hat she will wear to the party. At the last minute she decided why not wear one of her own hats, it would be good for business, and so she has stitched a stuffed cactus wren to the crown and added some silk lilac and is sewing feathers around the brim and a black veil and some sequins and silk roses in the mesh of the veil. She likes the idea that she will be veiled and somewhat mysterious since this is her mood or at least it's who she would like to be in this, the next chapter of her life. Also, she is fearful of catching typhoid, and the veil will cut down on contagious possibilities. And just as she is adjusting the feathered brim in the mirror, she discovers something she could swear was not there before, which is a row of tiny pearl eggs. Que Buenos! she says. A miracle! And as she leaves for the party, because the Parroquia bells are chiming which means she is already late, a little strand of tan yarn sprouts from the back of the hat and twists itself into a long braid, another miracle. But this she doesn't see.

———

If there's one thing I loathe and despise, says Julian, who is drinking whiskey from a silver tumbler which belonged to his grandmother, it's magic realism. It's so tacky, so utterly hackneyed and banal, wouldn't you all agree? He says this to the room at large, which is now full of improbable, inappropriate events. It's bad enough that it should permeate literature, he continues, but why my party? Above his head and slightly to the right, De De is flying by drinking a Corona and talking incessantly, only she has to shout a little to get attention. Señora, watch the chandelier if you don't mind, Julian tells her.

Dr. F. is sitting gloomily with a plate of hors d'oeuvres and he is licking his fingers. He hates this spectacle of his wife flying around the room in those ugly wings. Really, they look mangled and flea-ridden at the tips. Also their color is not precisely white, more like some old laundry.

De De is saying, I'm quite comfortable really, you wouldn't believe how natural this feels. And from up here I can see auras better. Carla, yours is silver. Oh no, it's the hat, the hat has some silver thing spilling out of it! How did you do that, Carla?

Because Carla's hat has not stopped manufacturing itself and truth be told is getting a bit unwieldy. In addition to the braided tail, there are now tufts of leopard fur, a giant milagro of a foot, and now this turbulence like tin foil crinkling up the sides. I wish you'd take it off, says Julian. It looks ridiculous. But Carla has no desire to remove the hat. She has a sense that the hat is constructing a solution to her life and whatever it is, she wants to know it.

Meanwhile, Gabriel has finally arrived with his beautiful woman who is immediately surrounded by a sea of men offering her drinks and food and their chairs. She does nothing but smile serenely at them with her small, white teeth and her eyes are pools of blue, like lakes. And her hair is the color of the gold damask tablecloth Julian inherited from his uncle.

And Lupe is passing around glasses of champagne on a tray, just like a '30s movie, and this is the only thing that, at the moment, gives Julian pleasure.

Because the party is not going as it should go and now enters the former Miss Americas with her husband, the tire magnate, and she is laughing uncontrollably. And the tire magnate is explaining that his wife began laughing for no reason about four hours ago and hasn't stopped. Even in her siesta? someone asks. Si, says the tire magnate. And she won't go to a doctor.

There's something in the air, says Maestro, some factor that's delicately rearranging the molecules. This isn't the first time in history that such a thing has occurred, you know.

Amazingly, everyone pays attention. When were the other times, Maestro? asks Carla, who usually has no patience for the Maestro, but at the moment finds him fascinating, even crucial.

I regret, says the Maestro taking a mushroom from a brown bowl, I have no facility for dates. But you can look it up yourself in the library.

What a load of crap, says Julian. Zack and Jessica are on the loveseat in the corner and she is stroking his head and he is closing his eyes. What's with those two? asks Julian. I thought they had parted ways.

Everyone is beginning to learn that all things are possible, says the Maestro. Which must be true because at this minute Gabriel is talking not to the most beautiful woman in the room, his date, but to Carla who in her outlandish hat looks more like a Oaxacan village than a human being. And he is saying, I would like to invite you somewhere after the party. Maybe we could drink some rum.

But just then De De shouts from her great height and points out of the window. Look! she says. The birds are changing before our eyes!

And it's true, one by one, the ugly birds with green feet are transforming into beautiful egrets. First they take on a transparency, a blur of silver imposed on their awkward bodies, erasing them, and then, in a dazzle, they become visible. White and flawless, they stand in the bare tree like stars. Even Julian holds his breath and takes it as a good omen. Because, amazingly, his shoulder has stopped aching and to prove it he raises his arm and points at the tree. If there's hope for those pinche birds, there's hope for all of us, he proclaims. And when he looks around the room it seems to him that many of his guests have the face of the handsome captain.

And Dr. F., from his place on the sofa, says, Say what you will, but everyone in this room is balanced, I have never seen such a thing in my life. There are no holes in any auras. Life, for the moment, is perfect.

And then we are all silent except for Miss Americas who is laughing so joyously it sounds like a symphony, but it is a symphony without the promise of closure. Otherwise, we would all applaud.

But we applaud later when Lupe brings out the cake made by Dr. F., which is chocolate and decorated with a miniature lake with tiny sailboats tacking back and forth. (How did this happen? Dr. F. asks the tire magnate.) And Julian cries a little, because he always wanted a sailboat as a child and because he has an urge to kiss Dr. F. on the mouth, and Carla cries because she thinks she is falling in love with Gabriel and how could this be? How is it that the affections are so easily displaced? And Gabriel says, You think too much, and when he looks over at the beautiful woman she is, to him, no longer quite so beautiful even though everyone else thinks so. At which point the little pearl eggs on Carla's hat begin to crack and a chorus of confetti bursts out of them and covers everyone like snow.

And the party goes on until 5 am at which point Elvira makes scrambled eggs and Sacha makes toast. And nobody ever wants to go home, but they do anyway, because human beings are programmed irrationally, which is to say habitually, and will always choose to honor convention rather than to endure, for any serious length of time, the sweet, unreasonable magic of their lives.

THE SWAYING SHADOW

NOW OUR SUITCASES ARE packed and we're waiting for the bus. Only the bus doesn't come until tomorrow. So we are waiting for time to pass because when a leave-taking approaches some part of us goes ahead to scout out the territory of the future and this leads to discomfort for the rest of us who watch one cloud which hasn't budged from its position over the pomegranate tree, off to the left of the yellow roof of the people with the red clothes hanging. The phone wire makes a blue shadow on a white dome and since it is swaying very, very slightly in a breeze, the shadow sways too. This is why I'm calling this story "The Swaying Shadow." I would like it to reflect a certain sorrow at saying goodbye as well as our restlessness. We have been here long enough. Magda has died. Gabriel has gone to Canada to visit his children. Miss Americas is having her baby. Zack gave us a plastic bag full of brass centavos before he left for LA and said: Poker money. The elections came and went without much fuss; last night someone mentioned the new Zapatista dolls that are for sale in Chiapas.

But at this moment, if we stop and think about it, a man called Raoul is making silver bracelets with the lost wax process in his little studio above the Mercado. From where he sits on a high painted stool he can see down through the green and red nylon awnings of the vegetable vendors to the vendors themselves, to their boxes of tomatoes and their blankets of tumbling wrinkled chiles, their garlic ristras, and crates of potatoes as small and red as the old pesos, and to the customers who stop and fill their bolsas. Sometimes he has to turn his own music up to drown out the noisy sounds of bartering and radio music. Sometimes—but not all the time—it distracts him. Then he might put on a Louis Armstrong CD or Quincy Jones. He might drink a Pepsi.

He might take something—say a pea pod, and split it open and sear it onto a waistband. He might have a conversation with a woman who is visiting his studio for the first time. Welcome, he might say. Only he doesn't say that. He is deeply shy and so is the woman who visits him. In fact, they can hardly bear to talk to one another. It's too nerve-wracking, two shy people in a small room. He shows her his jewelry samples, bracelets and pins in a glass case. She admires them, their weight, textures. Then he tells her about embryology, which was his first passion. He tells her about standing in a light-sealed room and watching sperms and eggs through a microscope. Some sperms, he tells her, are very lazy; they seem to be misguided, veering away from the egg or making their way towards it sluggishly, almost with indifference. While eggs are not merely passive, as she had thought, but rotate slowly while the sperms bang against their shells, wanting entry. There is one place on the egg, he tells her, where the sperm can enter and the egg has to present that side. It's very deliberate, he tells her.

This conversation makes her almost dizzy with anxiety. The implications are too crude for her fine-toned sensibility. He grins at her because he knows this and this knowledge makes him feel, momentarily, superior.

Do you want some water? he says. A Pepsi?

It's getting late, she says. I should probably leave.

Do you have an appointment? he says.

He would like her to stay, because in her shy nervous way she makes him feel less lonely. He would like her to stay the night and then stay there in his bed the next day and the next while he makes her pins and bracelets. She is not beautiful, but she has an awkwardness that attracts him. Also, she seems affected by what he has to say.

He tells her about a movie he has seen recently. In the film a man is married to a woman who torments him. He sets her up with his friend, a powerful personality, who she is instantly attracted to. The movie features the play of this threesome, this exchange of torment among them. In the end the woman is sitting on a pier in ripped clothes. It is a beautiful movie, he tells her. Very sensual.

The woman—not the woman in the movie, but the other—has some thought of leaving Raoul's studio. He makes her nervous. His jewelry is too expensive for her budget. Also she has to catch the bus in the morning, she is going back to the States after three months of vacation, if you can call it that. In retrospect—already she is thinking in retrospect—her time in this city is already being characterized by a vague, shallow quality. She did not manage to quit smoking. She did not fall in love. Also, she gained five pounds.

This Raoul is attractive, but weird. Melodramatic. Now he seizes her hand. What are your sexual fantasies? he asks her. Hmmm, she says. She is not impervious to this kind of question, but it's late. I must go, she says. Someone is playing a kettle drum in the Mercado. The shadow is swaying on the roof outside his window. It's been a pleasure, she says.

Let me make you a present, he says. Don't leave just yet, he says. His hands have little hairs across the knuckles; his nails are well-groomed, pinkish. He gives her a tiny silver dot. What is it? she says. What's it supposed to represent?

You can carry it in your pocket, he says. It represents nothing. Or it

represents anything you want. Eternity! he says dramatically. An ending!
Then he laughs.

This encounter sums up everything she's learned about this place—the
people, the architecture, the climate—and she fights to stifle a wave of
nostalgia. I shall cherish it, she says, rising to go.

Reconsider, he says. You can stay here. I will make you a belt buckle
with a snake. I have a sexual fantasy about snakes. There are so few women
with your intelligence. He says this to flatter her. He has no idea if she is
intelligent or not.

Maybe he is more perceptive than I give him credit for, she is thinking
(erroneously). Still, I must catch the bus. It's been a very great pleasure,
she tells him. She smiles warmly. She surveys his studio one last time—the
low table stacked with scraps of silver. The tangle of electric tools on the
floor near a basket of papier mâché fruit. His cracked coffee cup; his jar of
Cremora. His dark bedspread, his enormous sound system. The window
which frames the sky, the rooftop, the shadow which still sways bluely,
whose swaying she would like to imagine will go on forever, irrespective
of her noticing it. And Raoul too, soldering and twisting, thinking of
sperms and love.

Goodbye, she says. I won't forget you.

AUTHOR'S NOTE

I BEGAN THESE STORIES many years ago on my first months-long trip to the small city of San Miguel de Allende, in Mexico. I was with my youngest daughter Rachel, and I had never, before or since, known a place so beautiful and inspiring.

Part way through my writing, Rachel would suffer a serious injury that changed both of our lives— and so it would be many years before I was able to reenter the spirit of this book. There are some details here and there that do not conform to the current San Miguel—but because they were part of my original experience, I kept them. For example, telephone service was rare, as were televisions, so we had to betake ourselves to a particular café to use either.

Plus, the sophisticated technologies of today were not in existence anywhere when I began this project in the early 90s but came into existence as I wrote and revised through the years. Otherwise, the stories, old and newer, are meant to convey any time—then and now. These are tales, of a sort—not emblems of actual life but of an imaginative reality for which I am entirely to blame.

The characters portrayed in this book are fictional, but the real enduring magic of the city of San Miguel forms the heart of this collection.

It goes without saying that any errors of fact are my own.

Karen Brennan
Tucson, 2024

ACKNOWLEDGMENTS

"Bells" *TriQuarterly*
"Gabriel's Chair" *Gulf Stream Magazine*
"At the Fights" *Western Humanities Review*
"Zack" *Quarterly West*
"Julian's Birds" *Puerto del Sol*
"Sacha's Dog" *The Story Behind the Story*, ed. Barrett and Russo, W.W. Norton & Company

I want to thank all those who have supported this book, especially Beth Alvarado, Zita Ingham, and Steve Romaniello, as well as countless inspirational friends from long ago: Mikki, Suzanne, Karen A, Karen G, Rebecca, Paris, Masako, Tony, Christopher, Antonio, Tyler, Paulito and Raquel, to name just a very few.

I am incredibly grateful to Schaffner Press, Tim Schaffner and Sean Murphy, for having faith in this book and in me, and for their careful and helpful attention to these pages.

KAREN BRENNAN is the author of eight books, most recently, *Television, a Memoir*, a hybrid collection of micro-prose and flash pieces (Four Way Books, 2022). Among her other titles are the poetry collection, *The Real Enough World* (Wesleyan University Press), the AWP award-winning story collection, *Wild Desire* (University of Massachusetts Press), and the memoir, *Being with Rachel* (W.W. Norton). Her work has appeared in anthologies from Penguin, Norton, Greywolf, University of Michigan Press, Georgia Press, and Spuyten Duyvil, among others. A recipient of a National Endowment of the Arts fellowship and an AWP Award, she is Professor Emerita of English and Creative Writing from The University of Utah and teaches in the Warren Wilson MFA Program for Writers.